BENNY AND PENNY

THE BIG NO-NO!

A TOON BOOK BY

GEOFFREY HAYES

TOON BOOKS • NEW YORK

THE 2010 THEODOR SEUSS GEISEL AWARD WINNER

KIRKUS BEST CONTINUING SERIES

Make sure to find all the Benny and Penny books:

Benny and Penny in Just Pretend
Benny and Penny in The Big No-No!, **A GEISEL AWARD WINNER!**
Benny and Penny in The Toy Breaker
Benny and Penny in Lost and Found
Benny and Penny in Lights Out!
Benny and Penny in How to Say Goodbye

For Debby Carter

Editorial Director: FRANÇOISE MOULY

Book Design: FRANÇOISE MOULY & JONATHAN BENNETT

GEOFFREY HAYES' artwork was drawn in colored pencil.

A TOON Book™ © 2009 Geoffrey Hayes & TOON Books, an imprint of RAW Junior, LLC, 27 Greene Street, New York, NY 10013. No part of this book may be used or reproduced in any manner whatsoever without written permission except in the case of brief quotations embodied in critical articles and reviews. TOON Graphics™, TOON Books®, LITTLE LIT® and TOON Into Reading!™ are trademarks of RAW Junior, LLC. All rights reserved. The Library of Congress has catalogued the hardcover edition as follows: Hayes, Geoffrey. Benny and Penny in The big no-no! : a TOON Book / by Geoffrey Hayes. p. cm. Summary: Two mice meet their new neighbor and discover that she is not as scary as they feared. 1. Graphic novels. [1. Graphic novels. 2. Mice--Fiction. 3. Brothers and sisters--Fiction. 4. Neighbors--Fiction.] I. Title. II. Title: Big no-no! PZ7.7.H39Be 2009   [E]--dc22   2008036307. All our books are Smyth Sewn (the highest library-quality binding available) and printed with soy-based inks on acid-free, woodfree paper harvested from responsible sources. Printed in China by C&C Offset Printing Co., Ltd. Distributed to the trade by Consortium Book Sales & Distribution, a division of Ingram Content Group; orders (866) 400-5351; ips@ingramcontent.com; www.cbsd.com.

ISBN 978-0-9799238-9-0 (hardcover)
ISBN 978-1-935179-35-1 (paperback)

19 20 21 22 23 24 C&C 15 14 13 12 11 10 9 8 7

WWW.TOON-BOOKS.COM

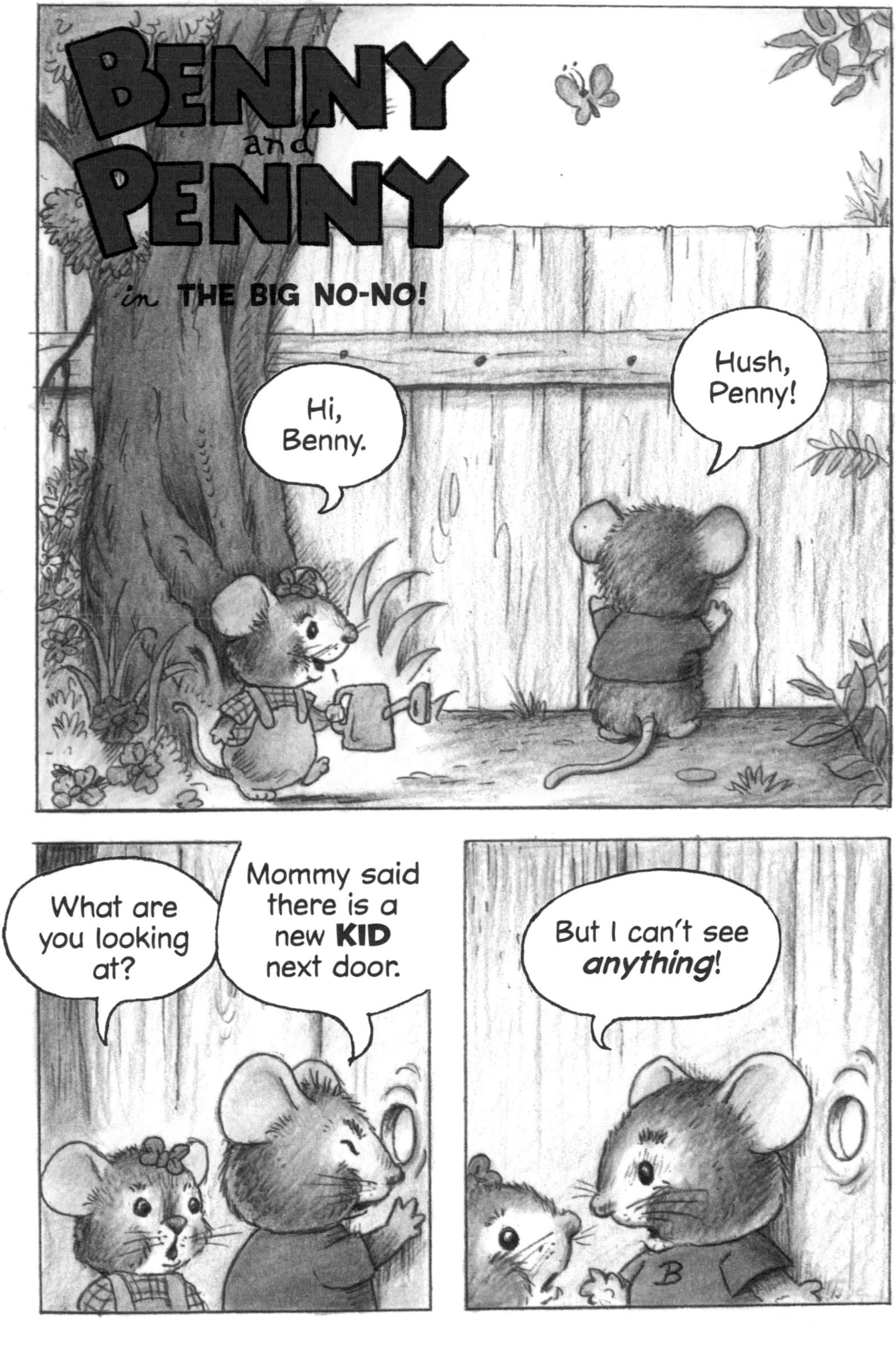
BENNY and PENNY
in THE BIG NO-NO!
Hi, Benny.
Hush, Penny!
What are you looking at?
Mommy said there is a new KID next door.
But I can't see anything!

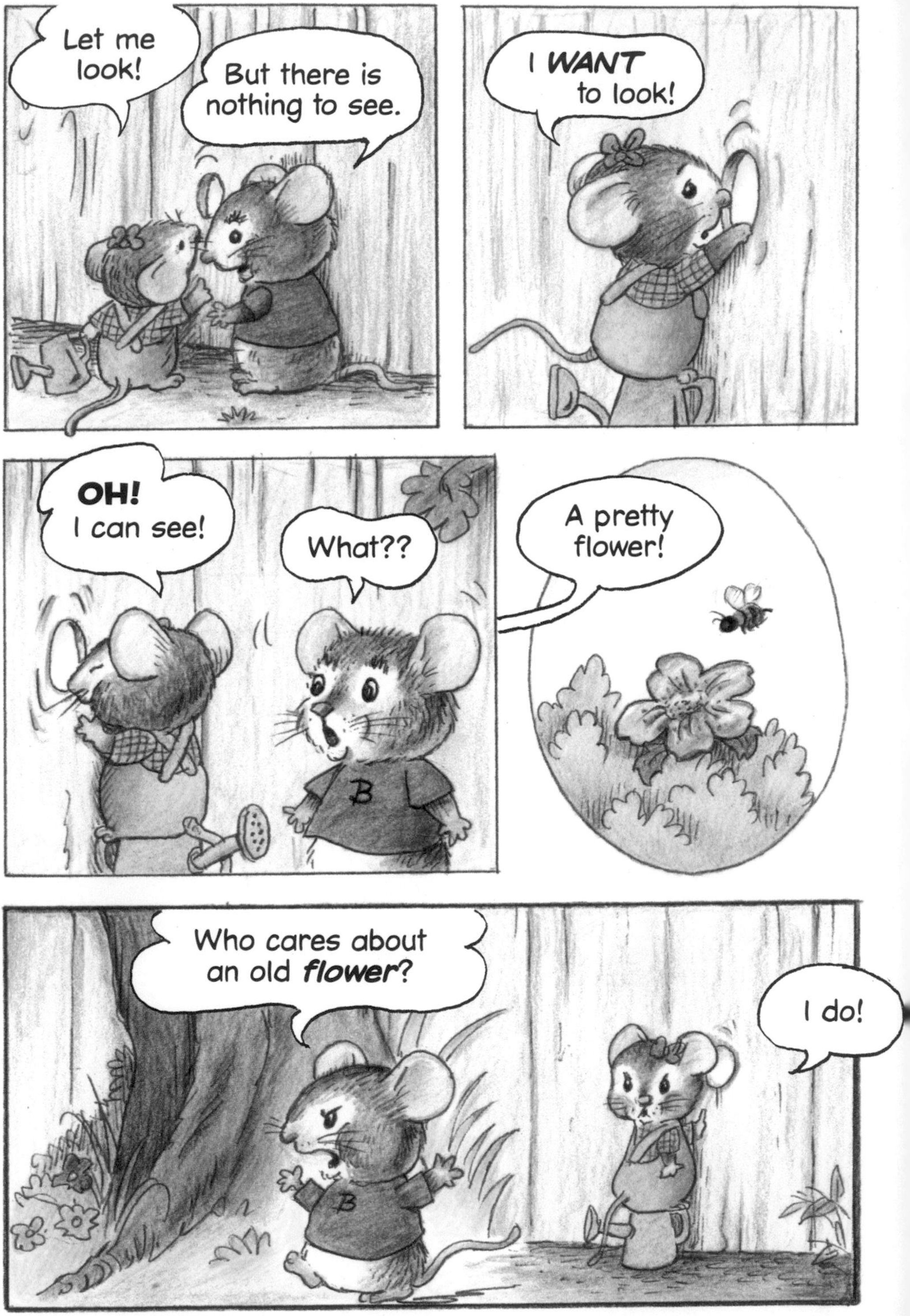

Let me look!
But there is nothing to see.
I **WANT** to look!
OH! I can see!
What??
A pretty flower!
Who cares about an old ***flower***?
I do!

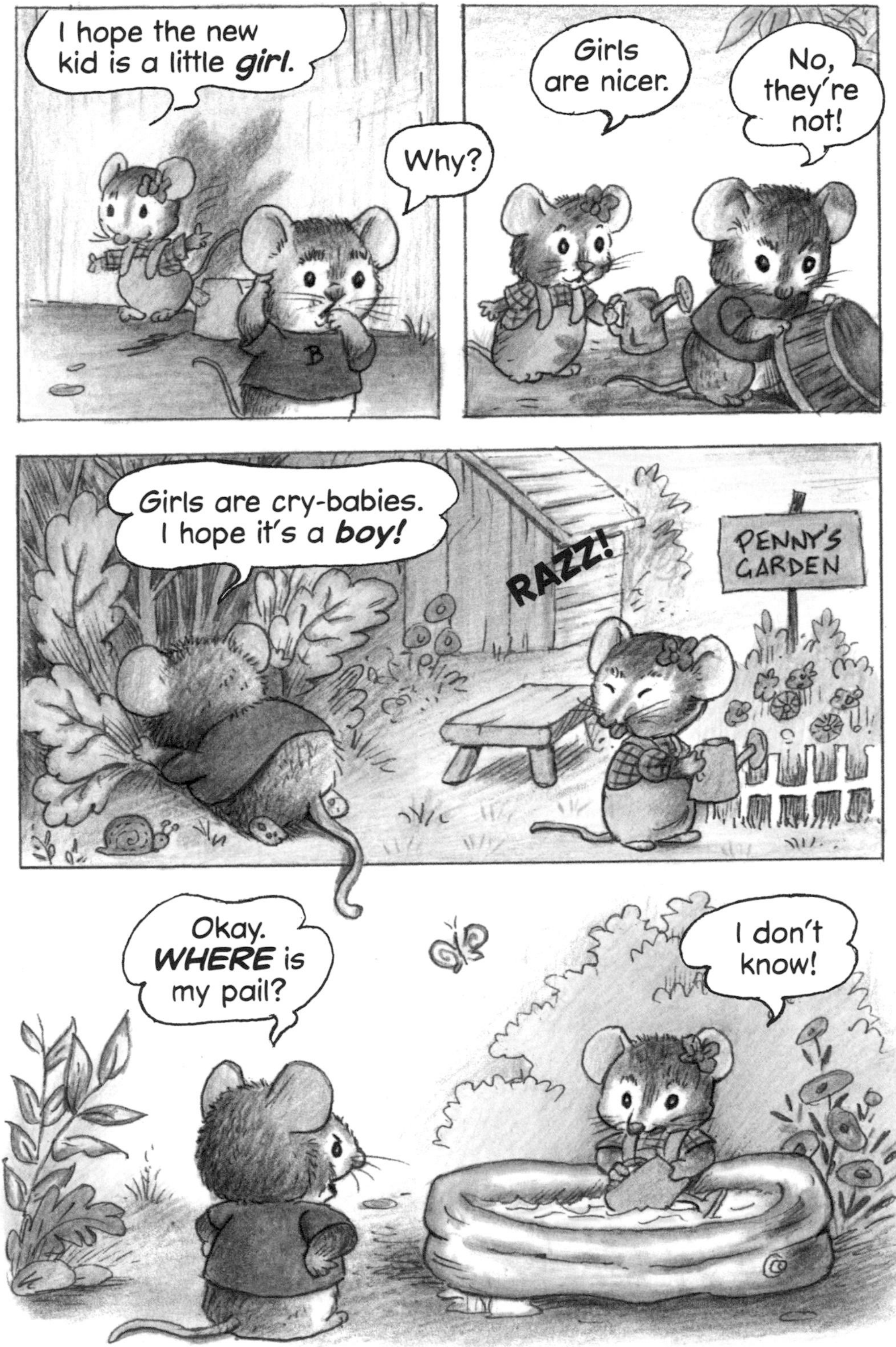
I hope the new kid is a little ***girl***.
Why?
Girls are nicer.
No, they're not!
Girls are cry-babies. I hope it's a ***boy!***
RAZZ!
PENNY'S GARDEN
Okay. ***WHERE*** is my pail?
I don't know!

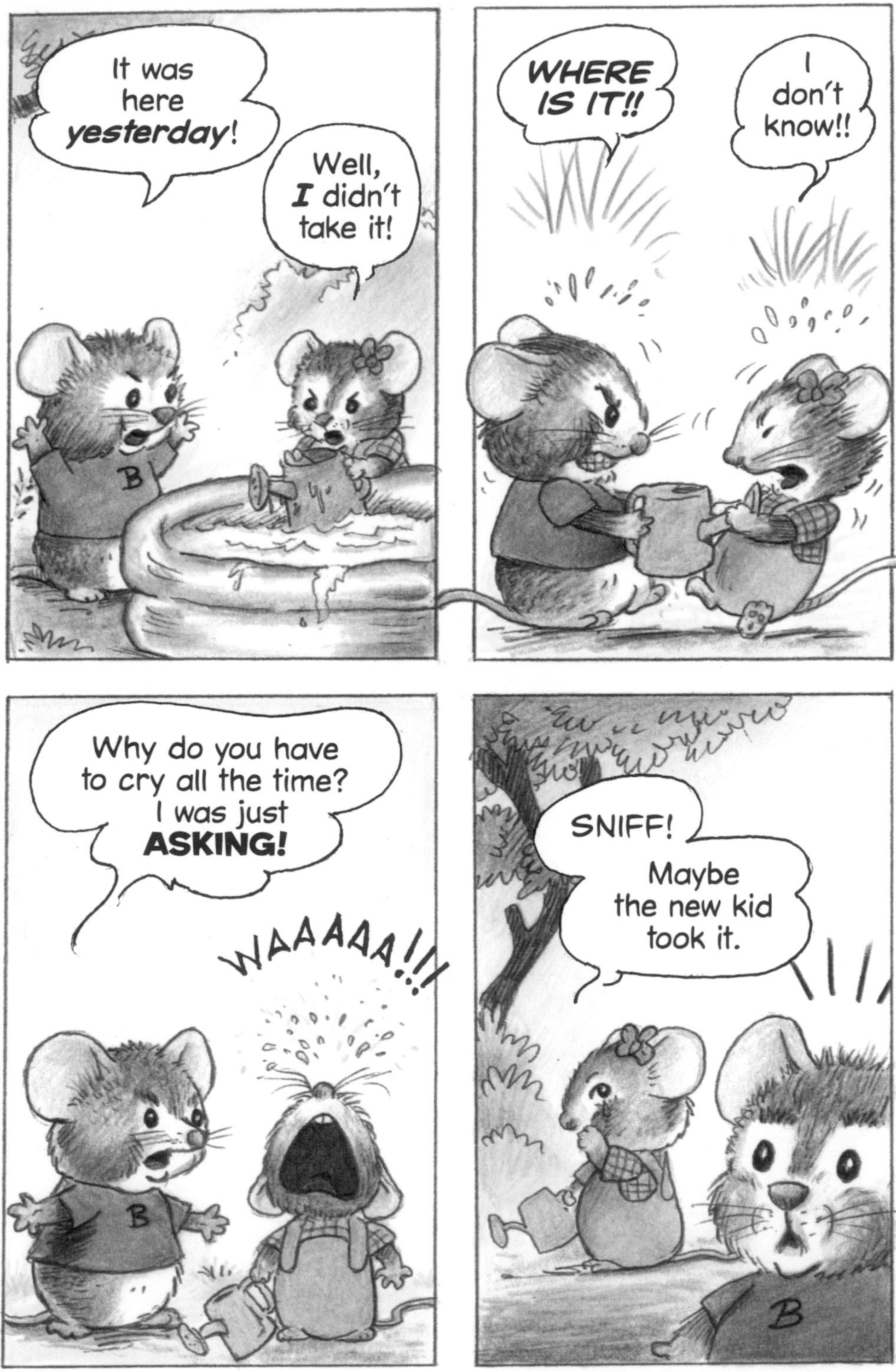
It was here yesterday!
Well, I didn't take it!
WHERE IS IT!!
I don't know!!
Why do you have to cry all the time? I was just ASKING!
WAAAAA!!!
SNIFF!
Maybe the new kid took it.

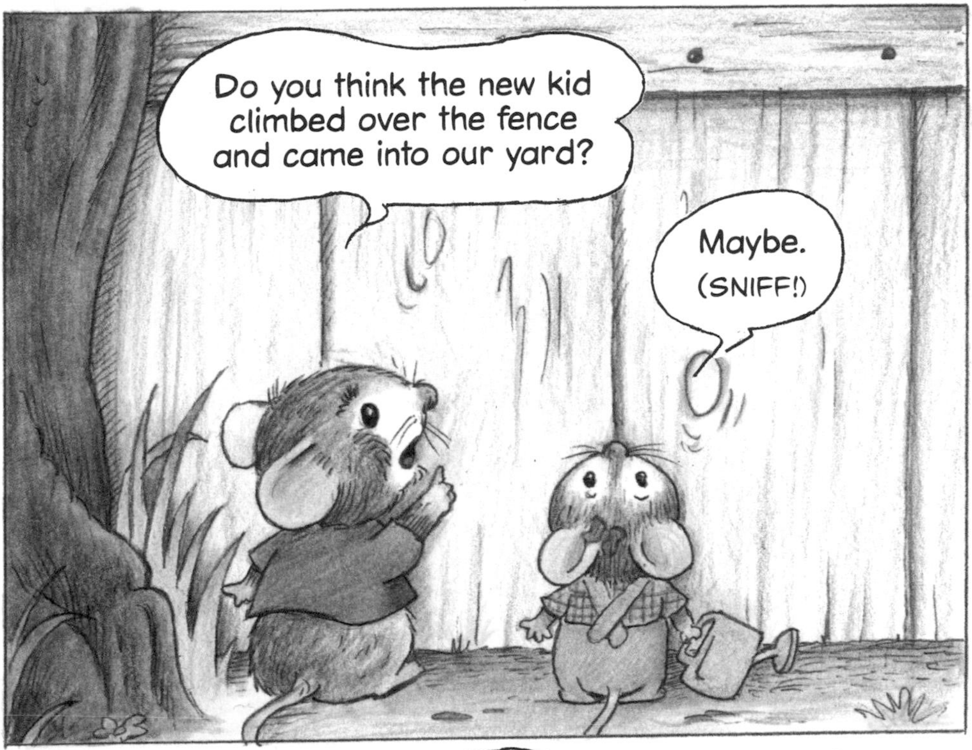
Do you think the new kid climbed over the fence and came into our yard?
Maybe. (SNIFF!)

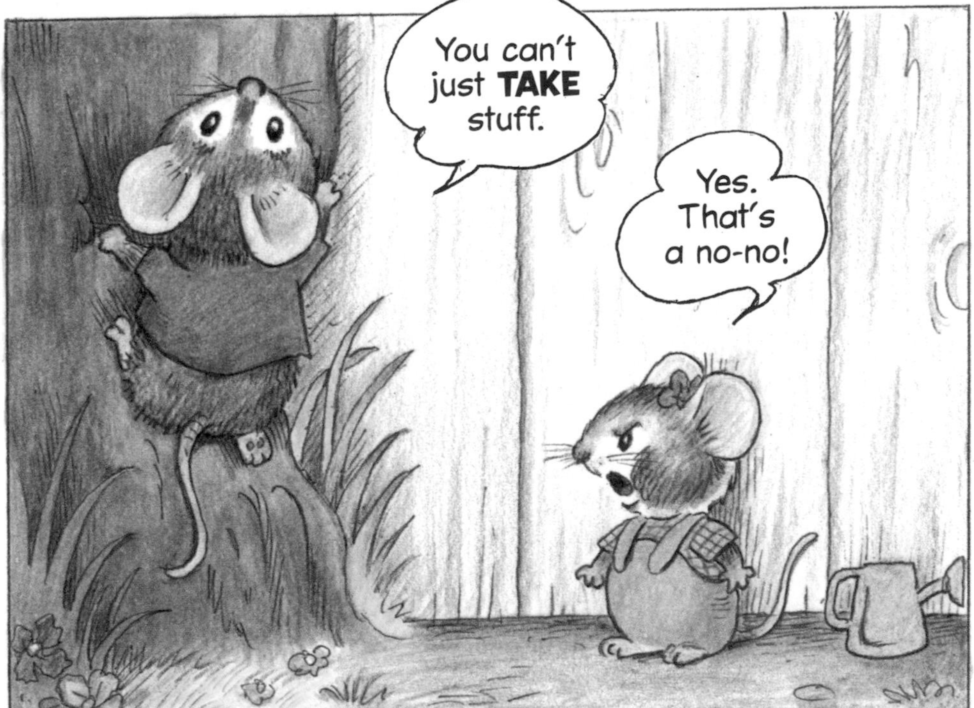
You can't just TAKE stuff.
Yes. That's a no-no!

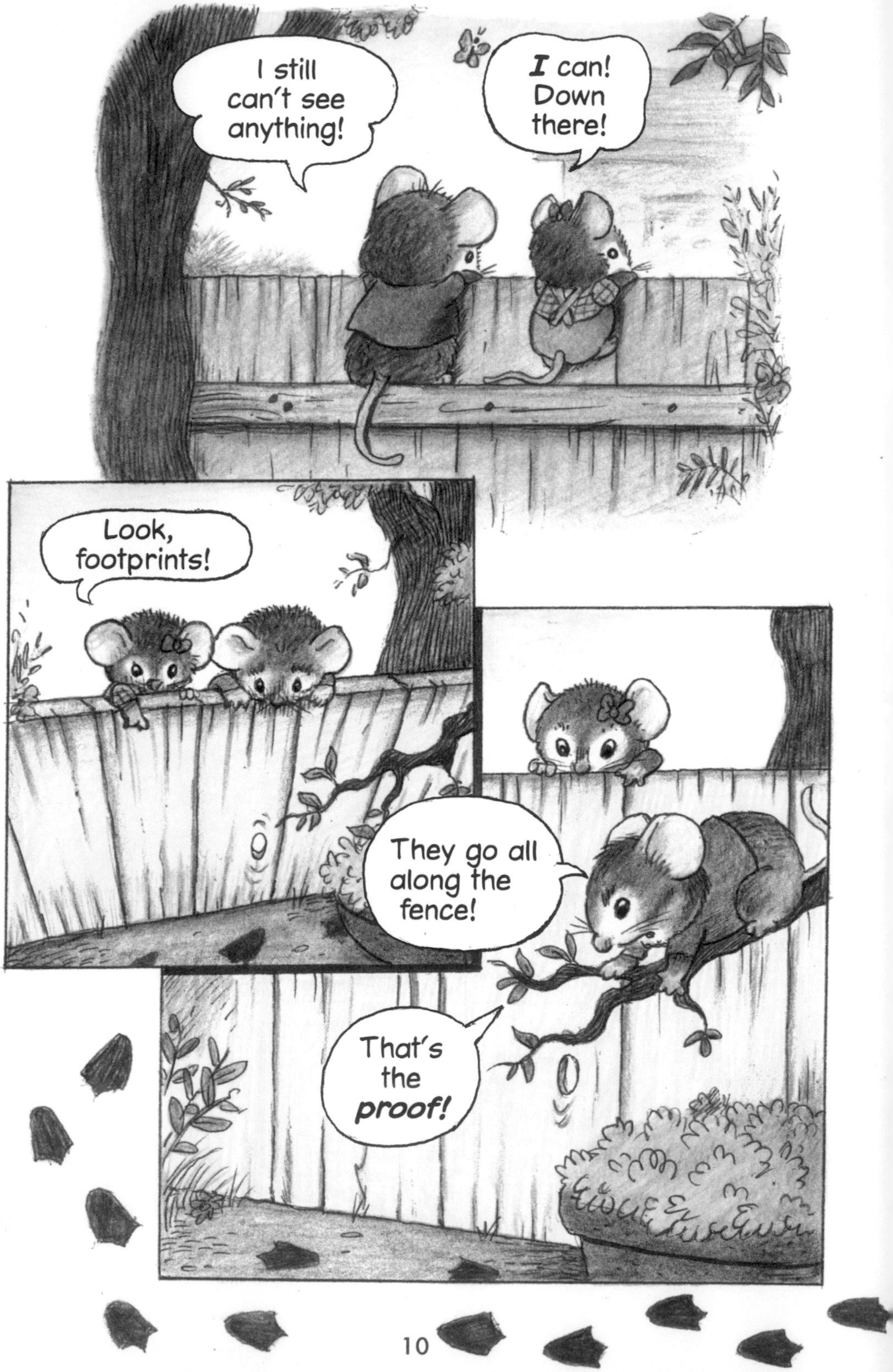

I still can't see anything!
I can! Down there!
Look, footprints!
They go all along the fence!
That's the ***proof!***

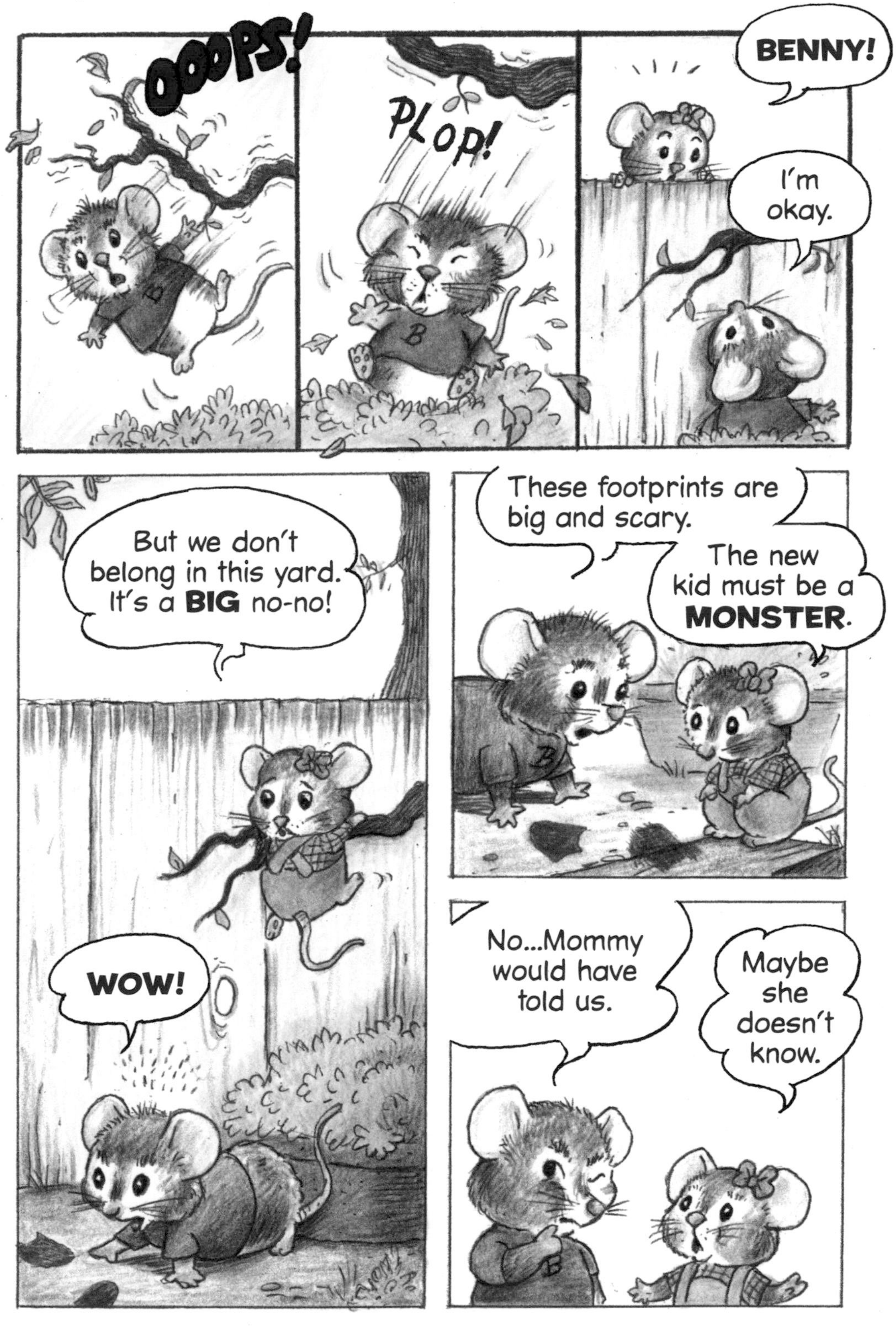
OOOPS!
PLOP!
BENNY!
I'm okay.
But we don't belong in this yard. It's a **BIG** no-no!
WOW!
These footprints are big and scary.
The new kid must be a **MONSTER**.
No...Mommy would have told us.
Maybe she doesn't know.

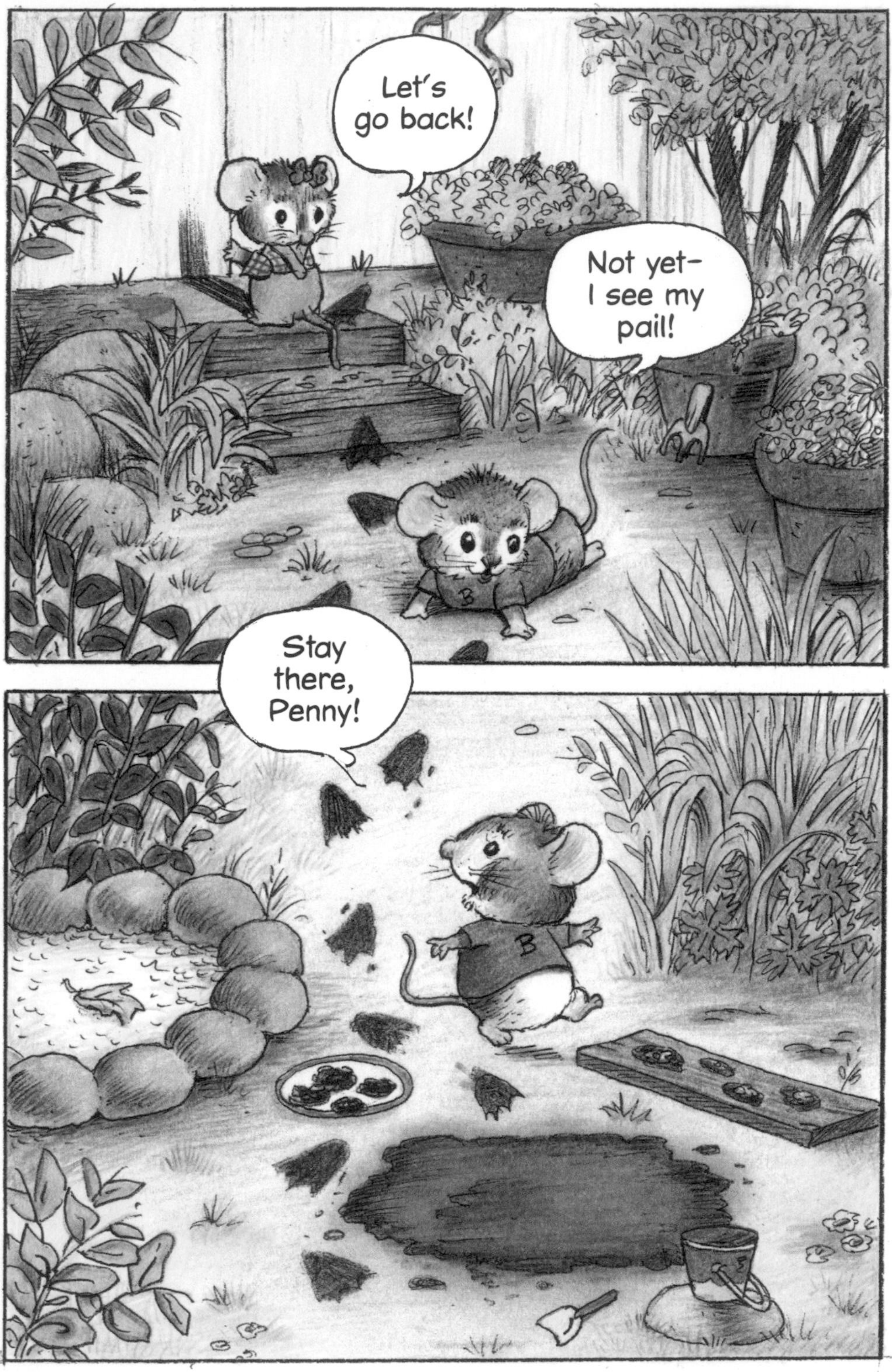
Let's go back!
Not yet-
I see my pail!
Stay there, Penny!

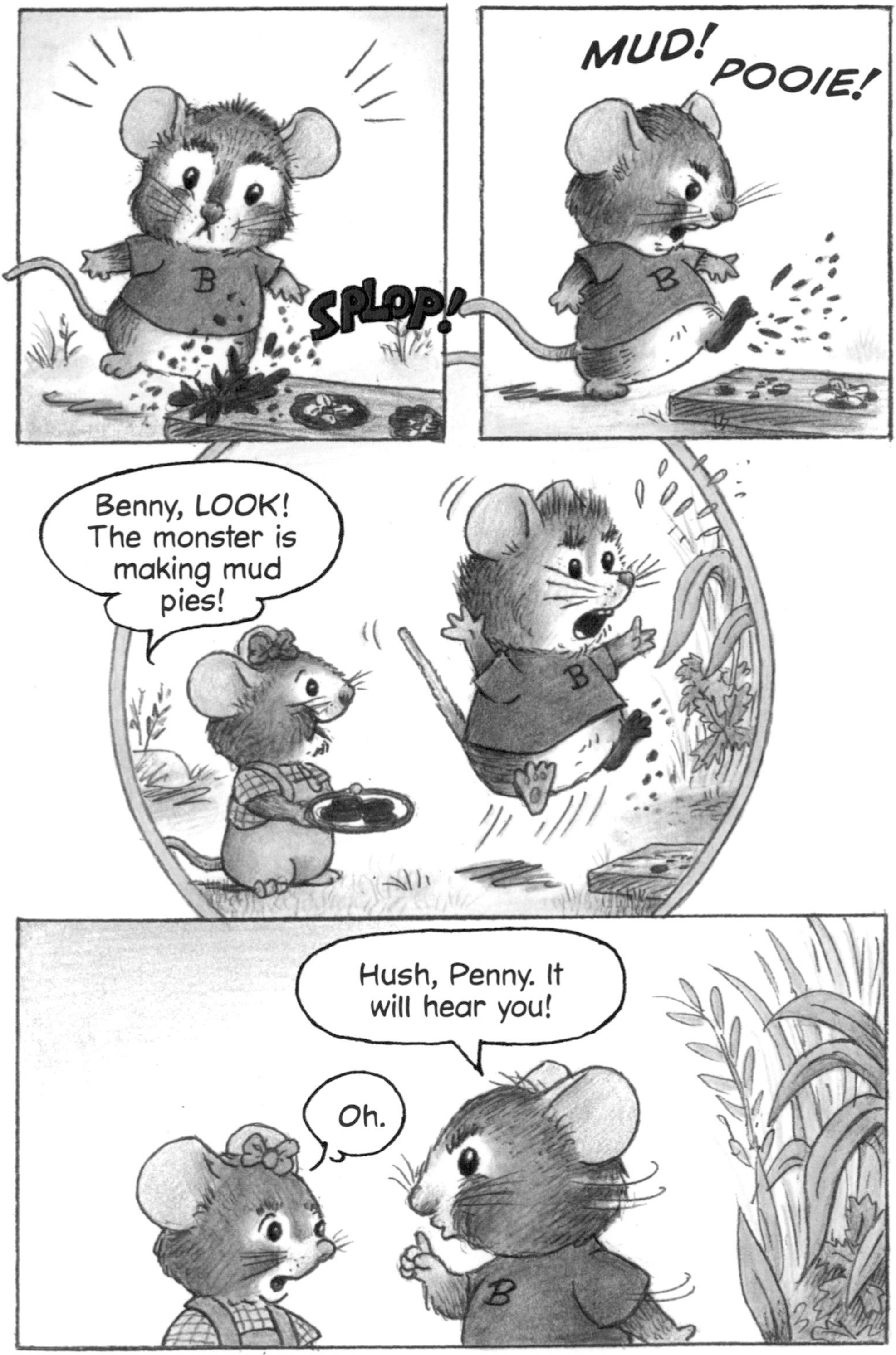
SPLOP!
MUD! POOIE!
Benny, LOOK! The monster is making mud pies!
Hush, Penny. It will hear you!
Oh.

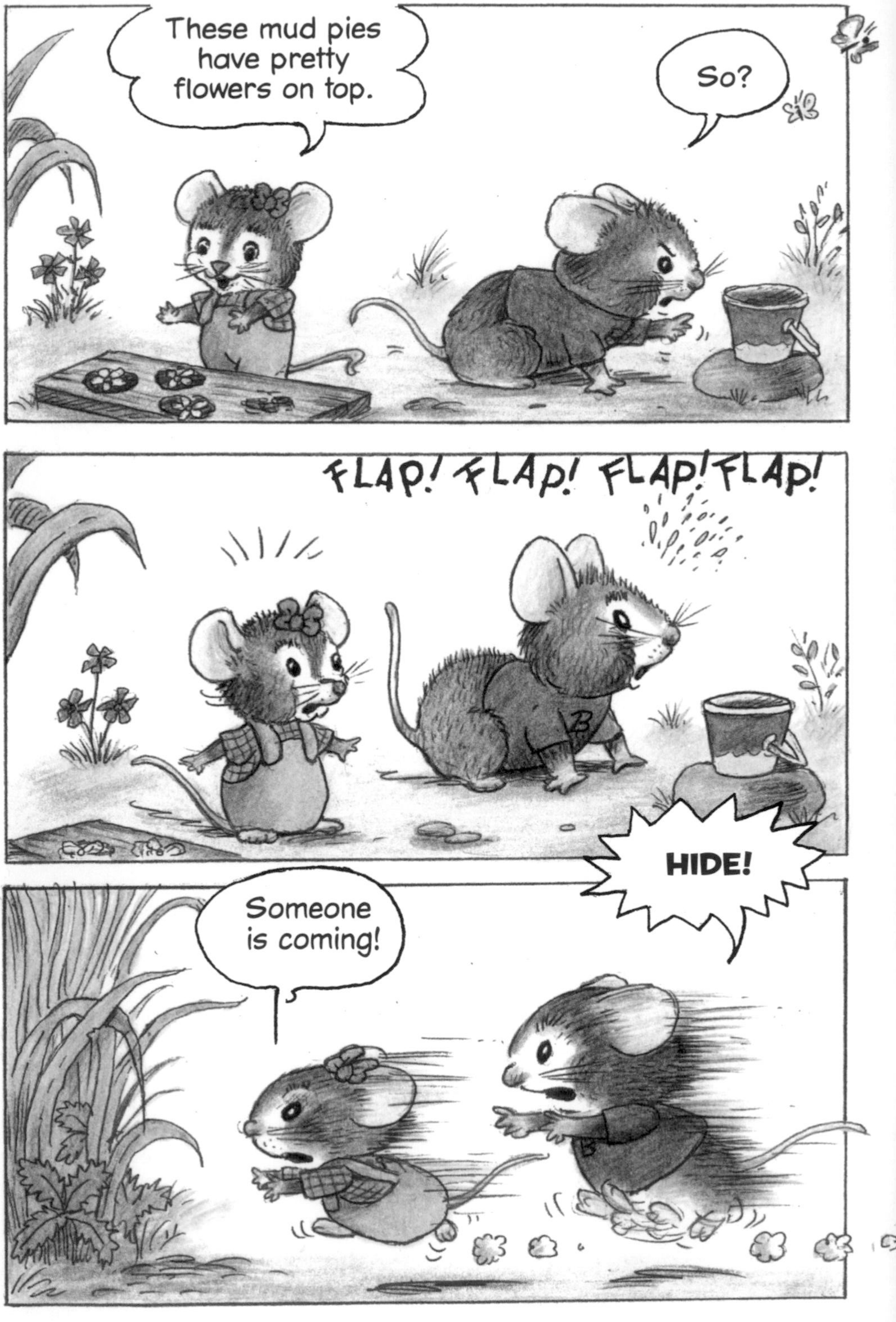
These mud pies have pretty flowers on top.
So?
FLAP! FLAP! FLAP! FLAP!
HIDE!
Someone is coming!

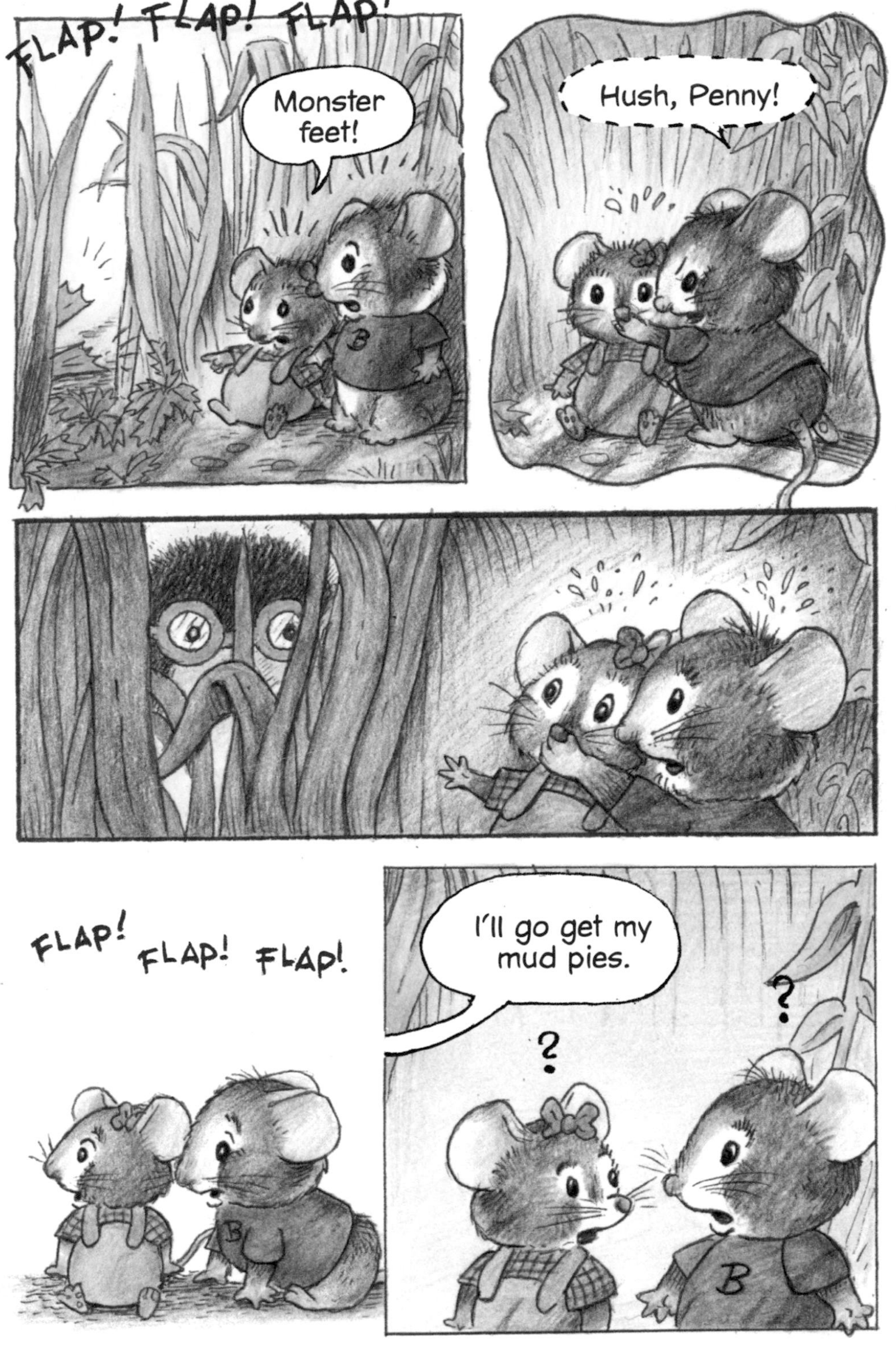
FLAP! FLAP! FLAP!
Monster feet!
Hush, Penny!
FLAP! FLAP! FLAP!
I'll go get my mud pies.
?
?

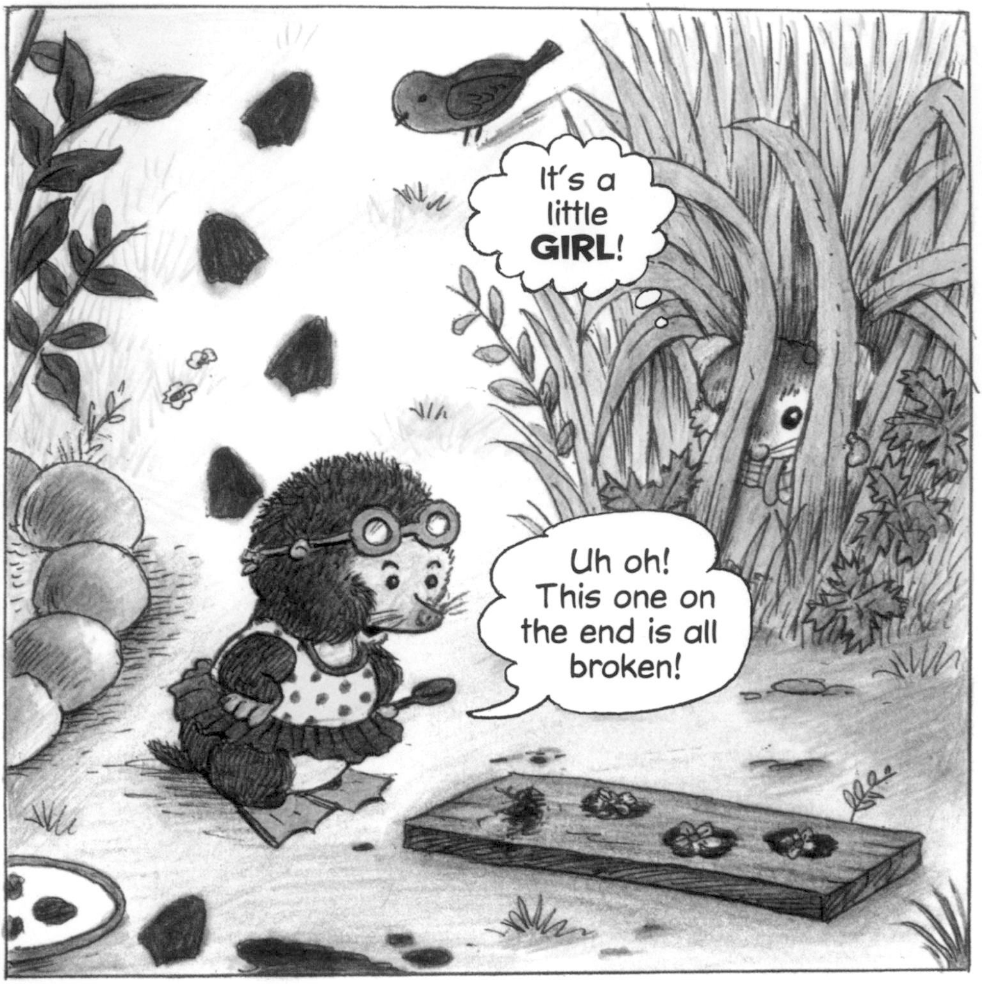
It's a little GIRL!
Uh oh! This one on the end is all broken!

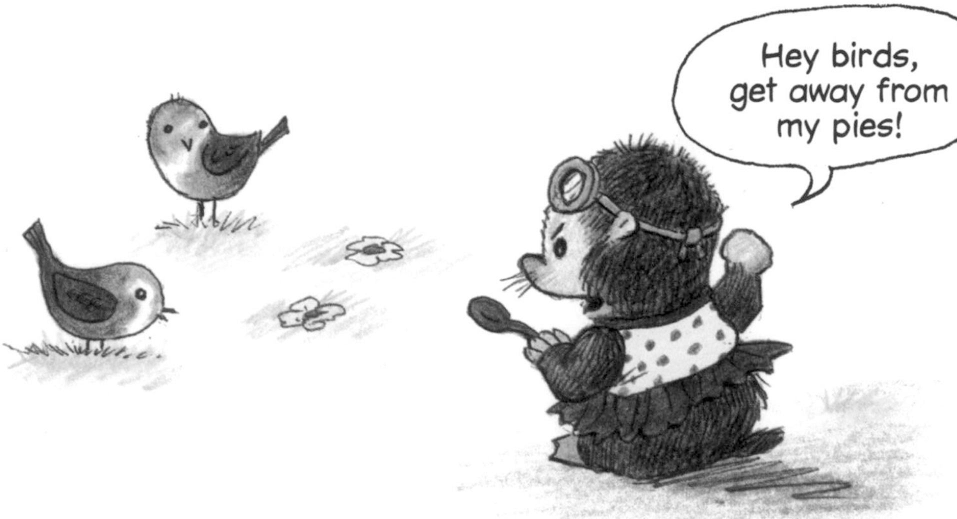
Hey birds, get away from my pies!

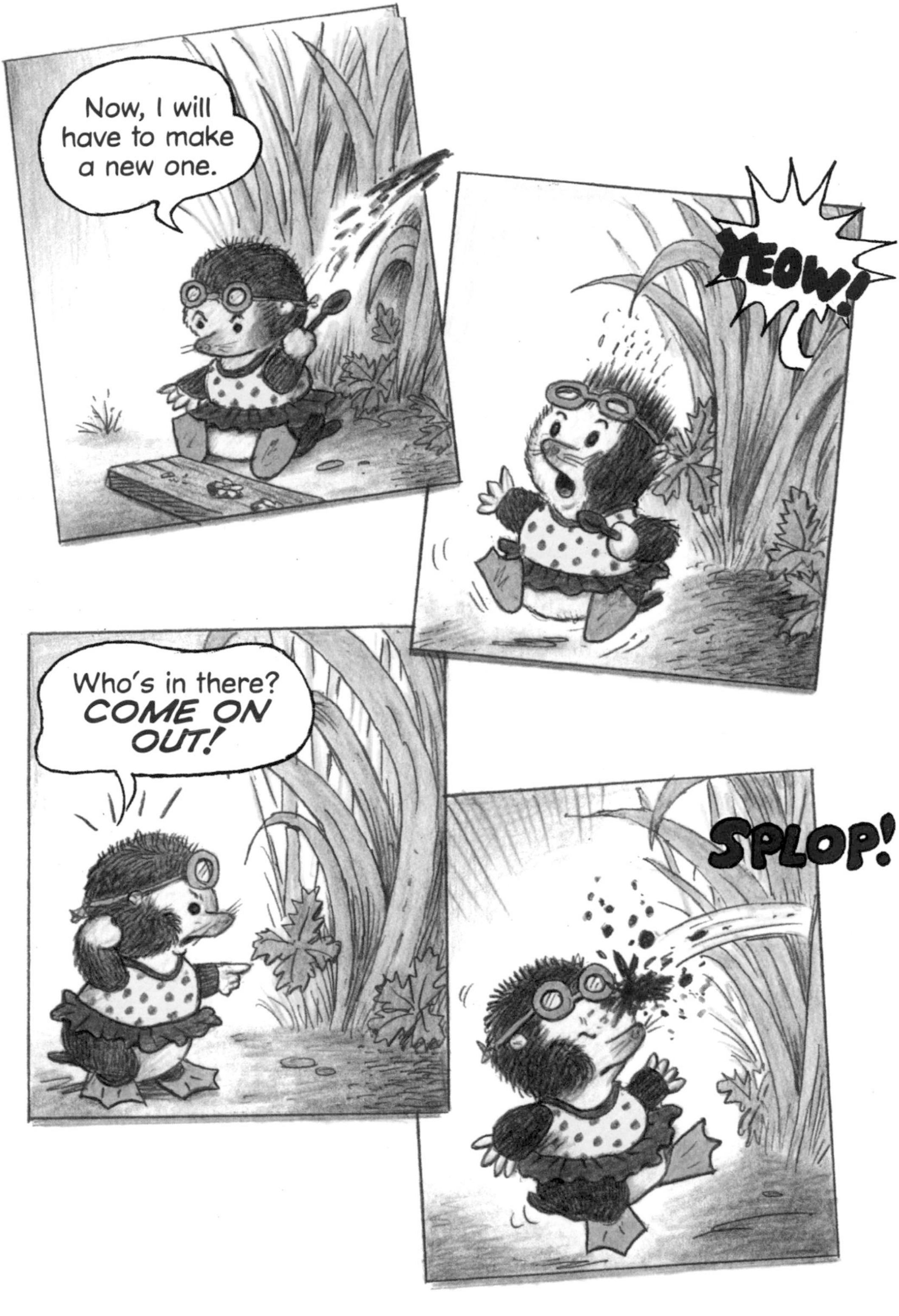
Now, I will have to make a new one.
YEOW!
Who's in there? COME ON OUT!
SPLOP!

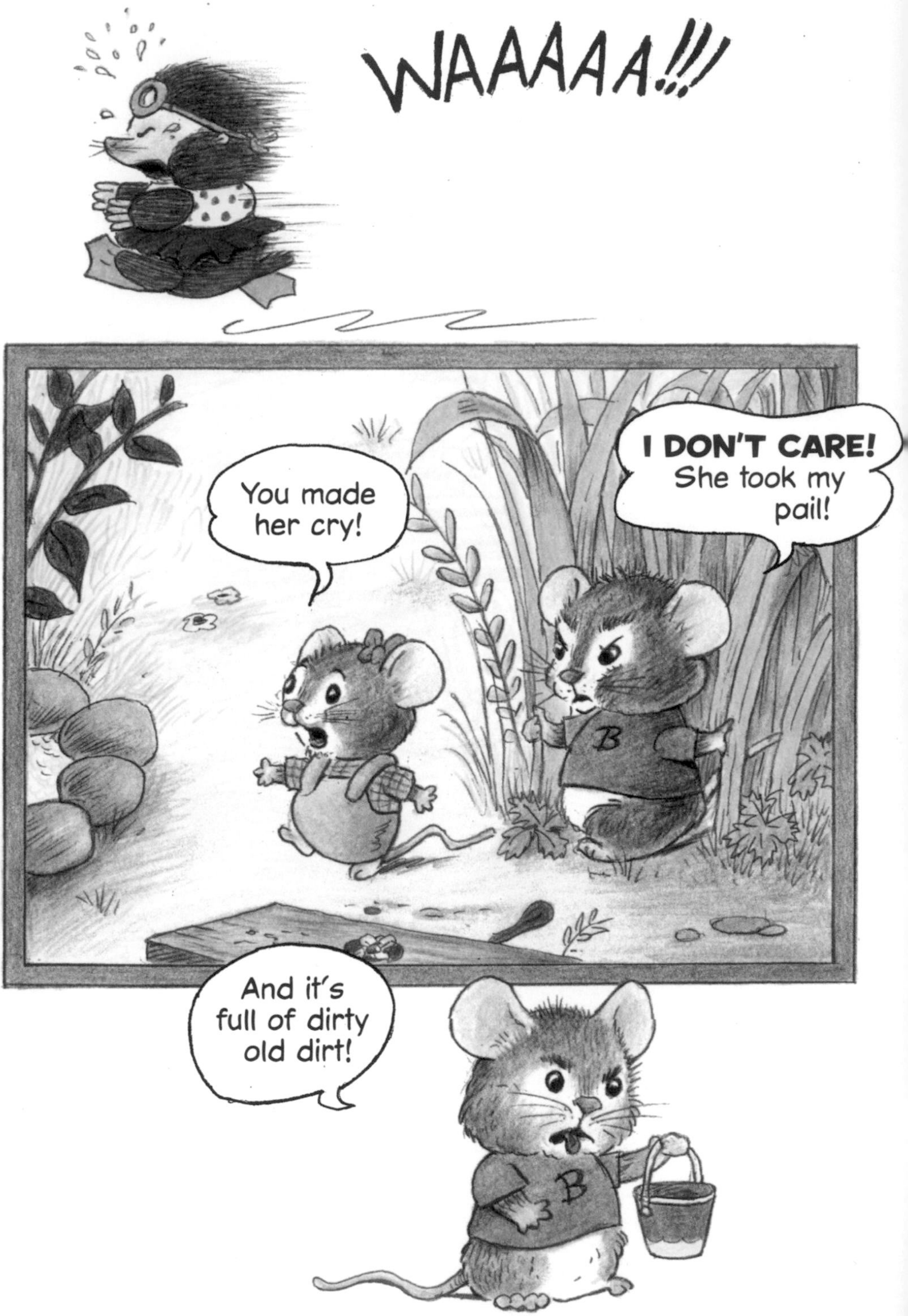
WAAAAA!!!
You made her cry!
I DON'T CARE! She took my pail!
And it's full of dirty old dirt!

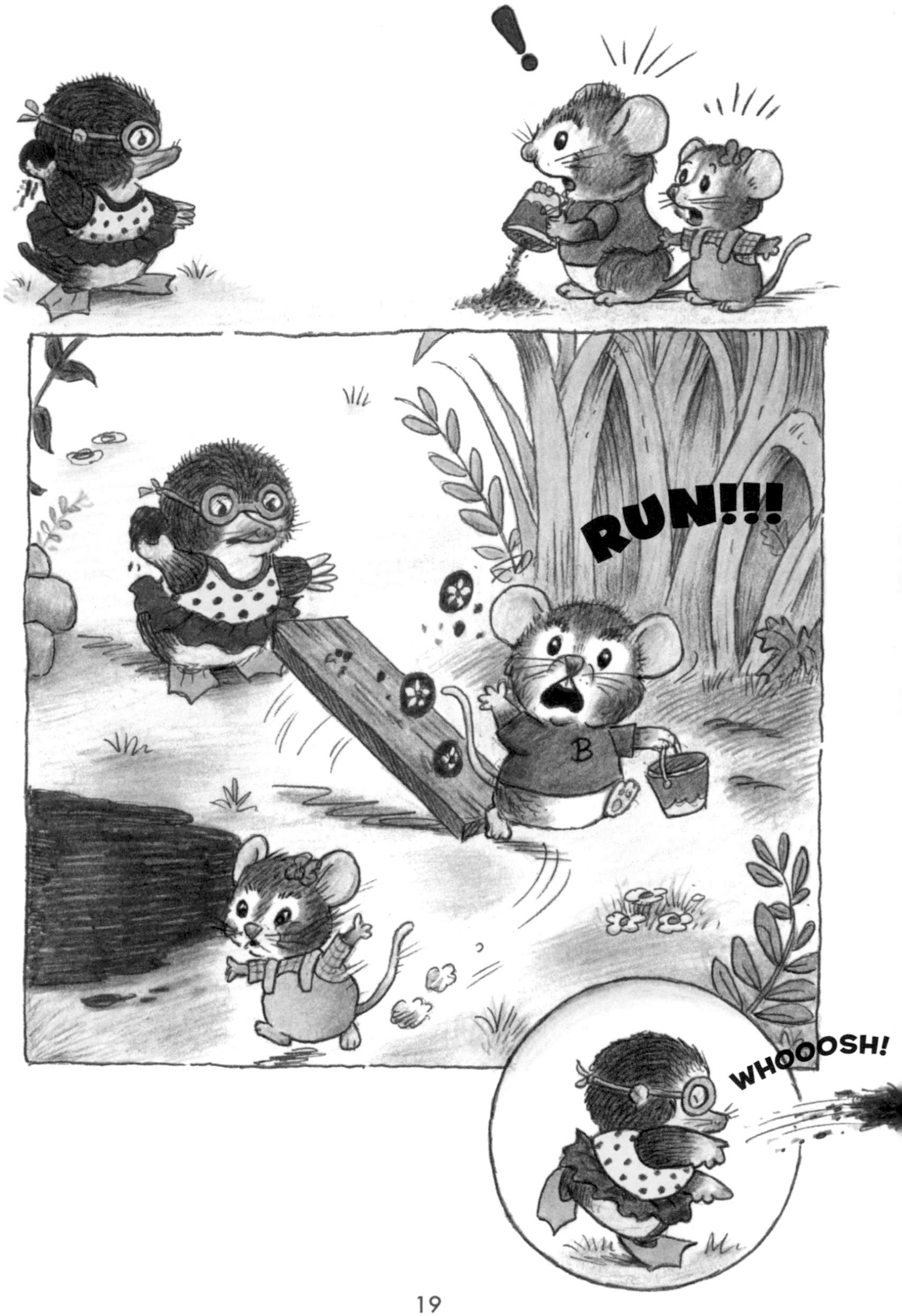
!
RUN!!!
WHOOOSH!

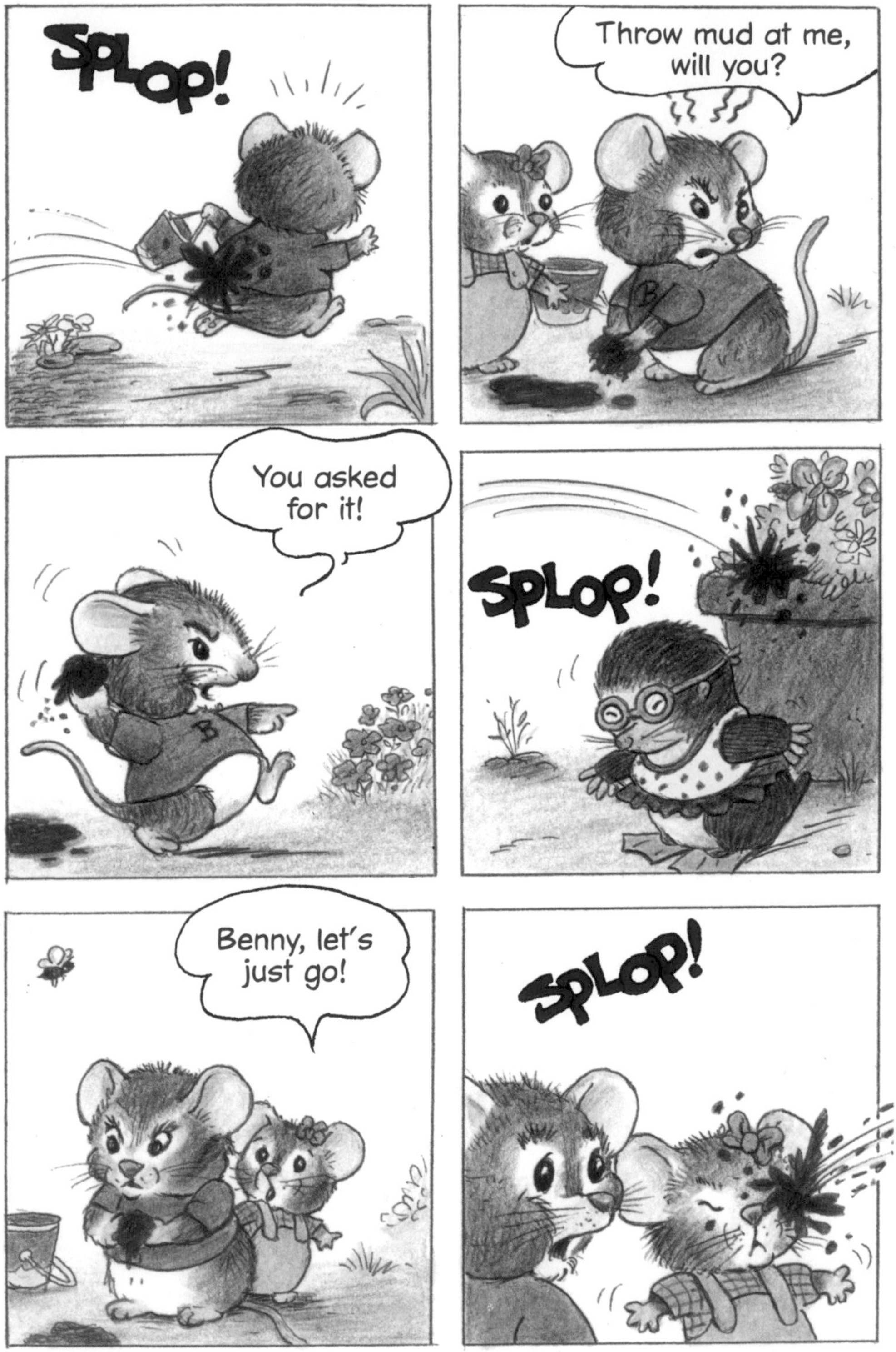
SPLOP!
Throw mud at me, will you?
You asked for it!
SPLOP!
Benny, let's just go!
SPLOP!

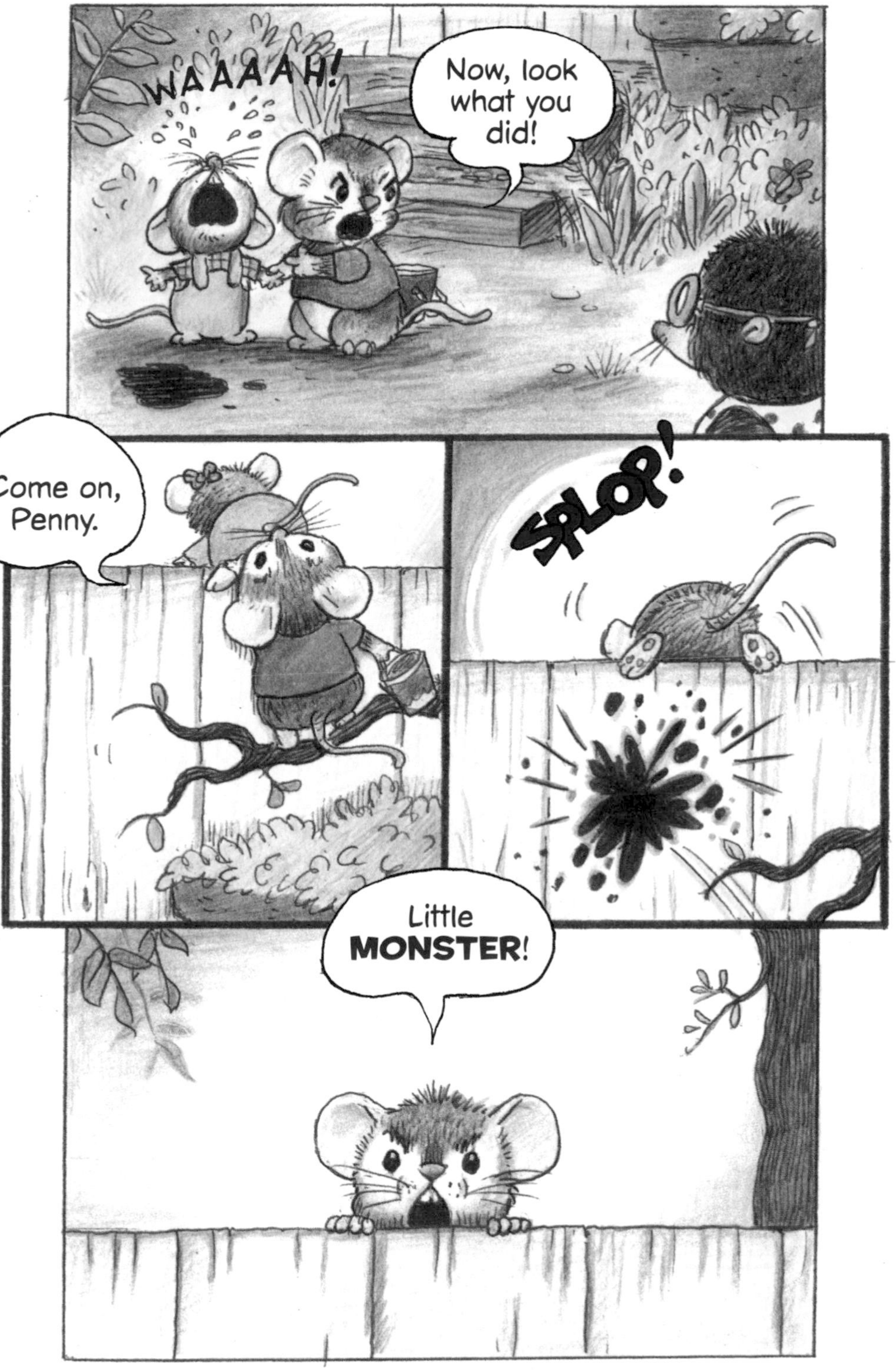
WAAAAH!
Now, look what you did!
Come on, Penny.
SPLOP!
Little MONSTER!

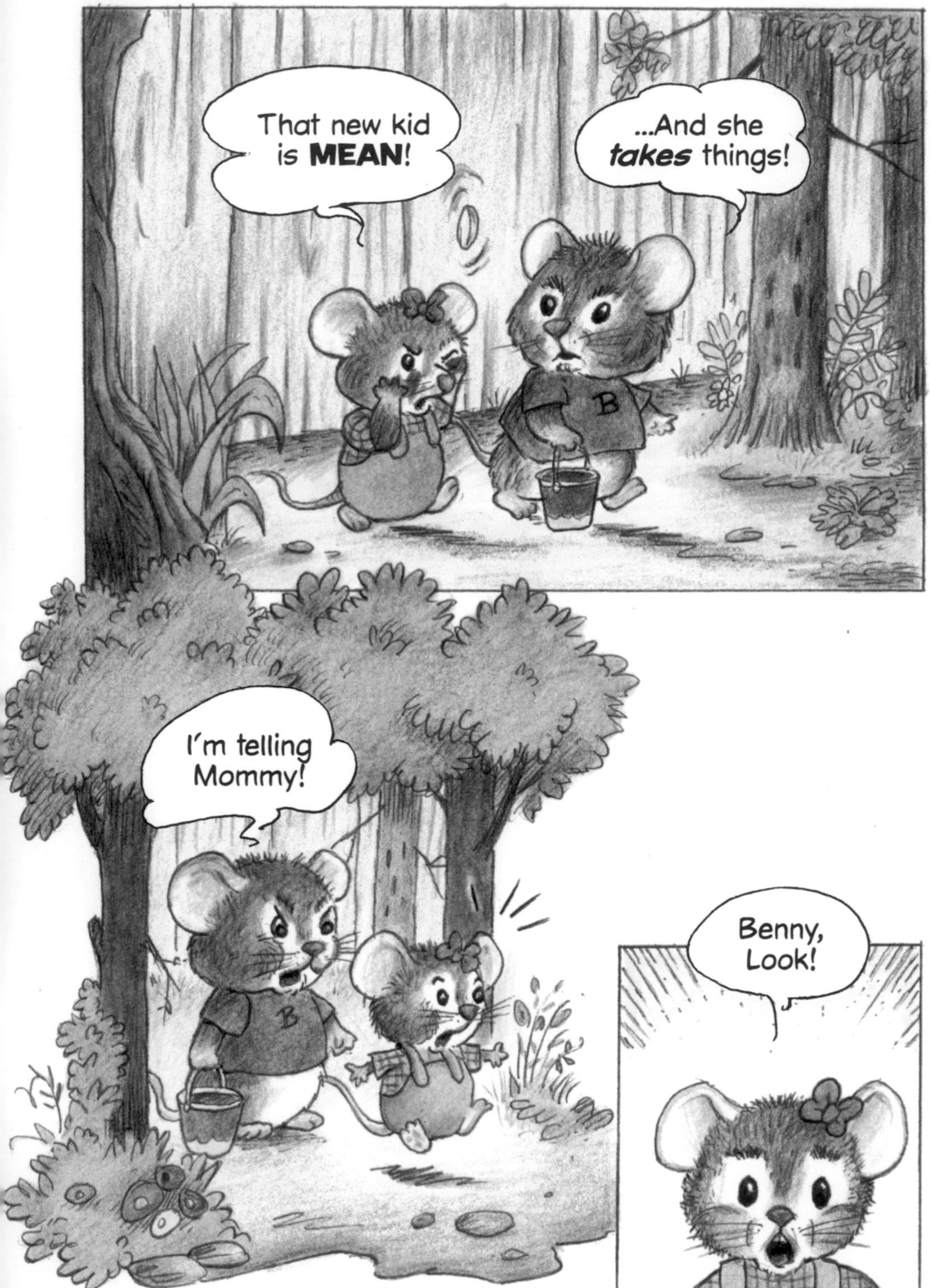
That new kid is **MEAN**!
...And she *takes* things!
I'm telling Mommy!
Benny, Look!

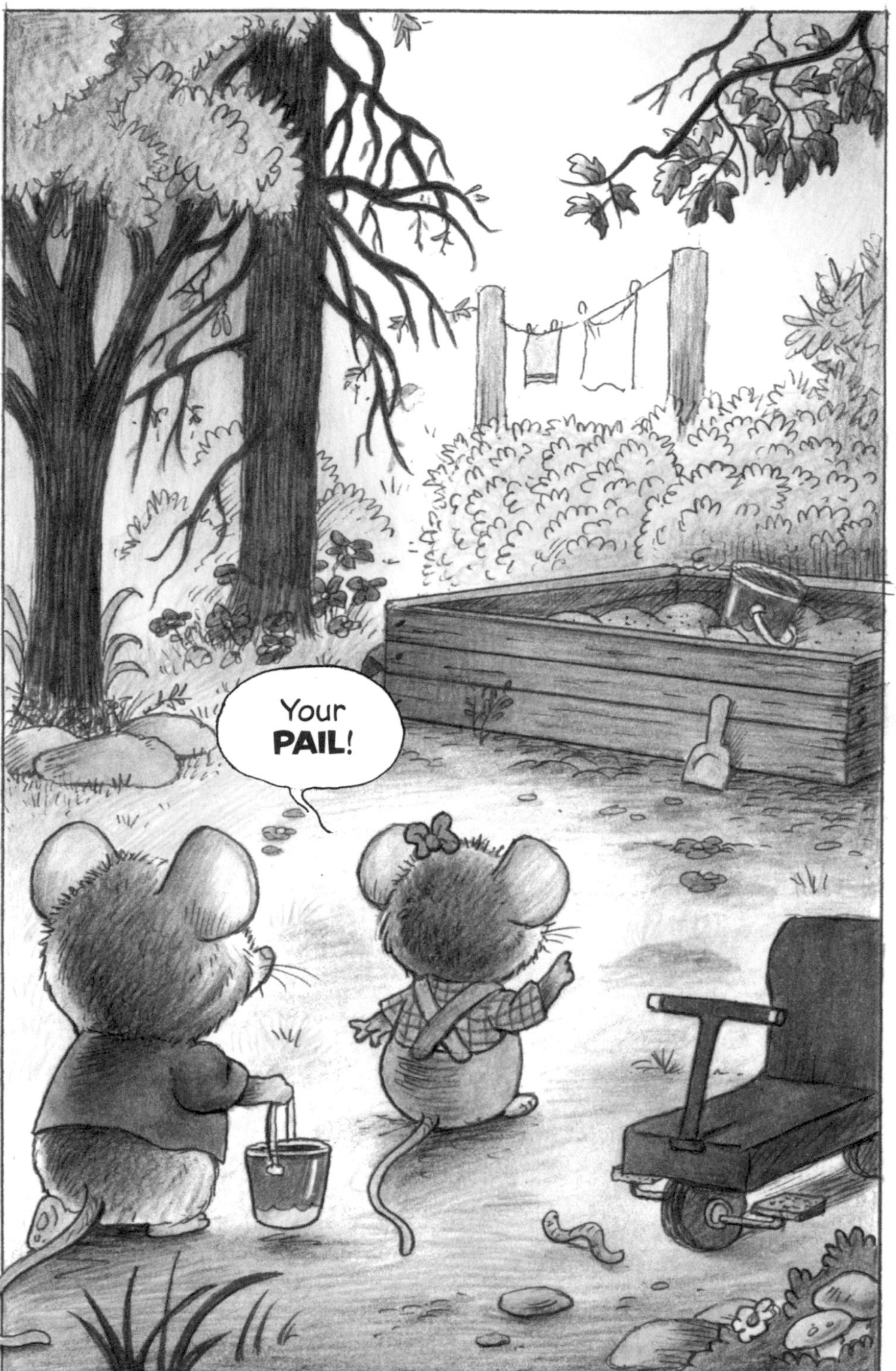
Your
PAIL!

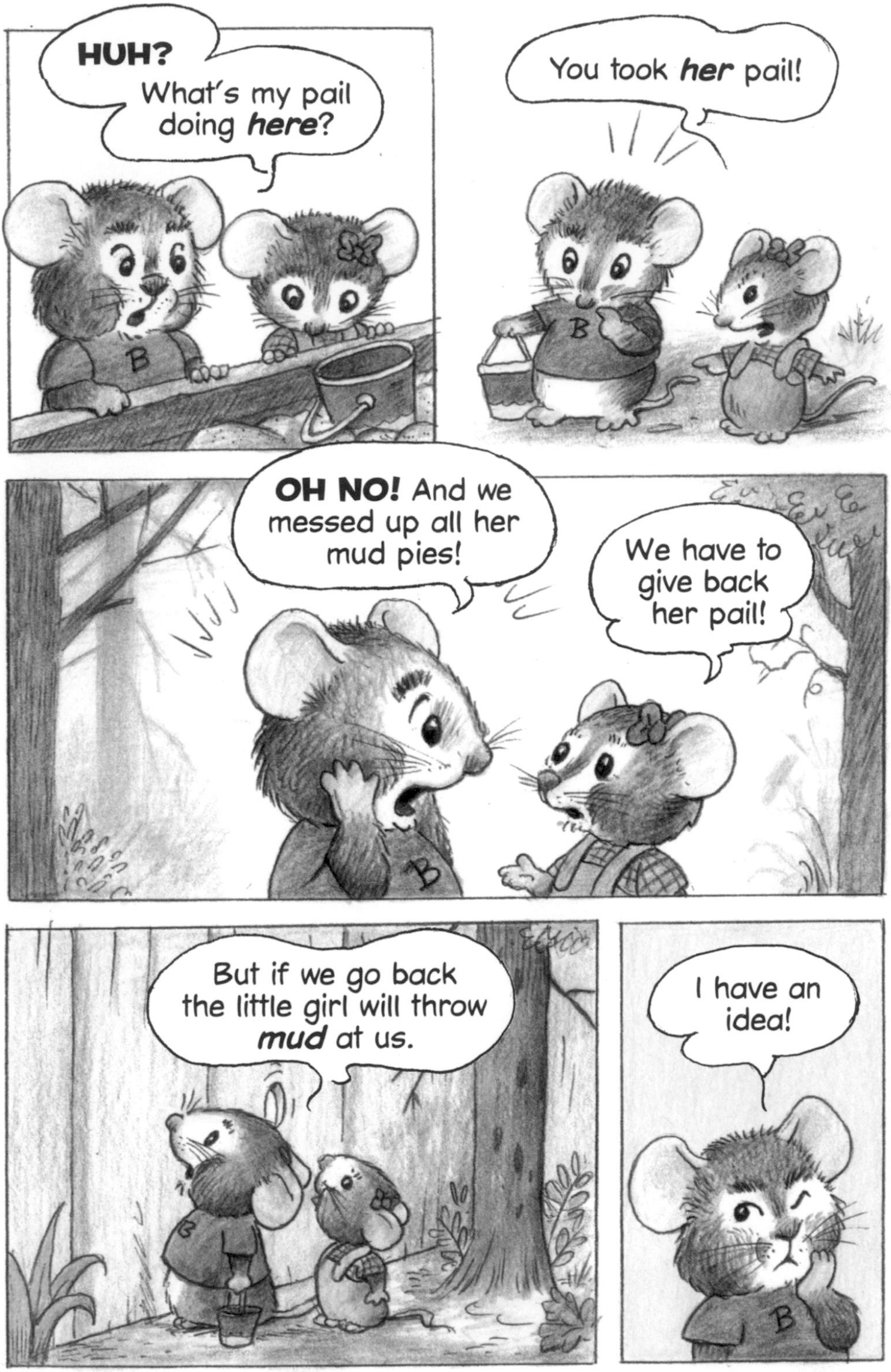
HUH? What's my pail doing *here*?
You took *her* pail!
OH NO! And we messed up all her mud pies!
We have to give back her pail!
But if we go back the little girl will throw *mud* at us.
I have an idea!

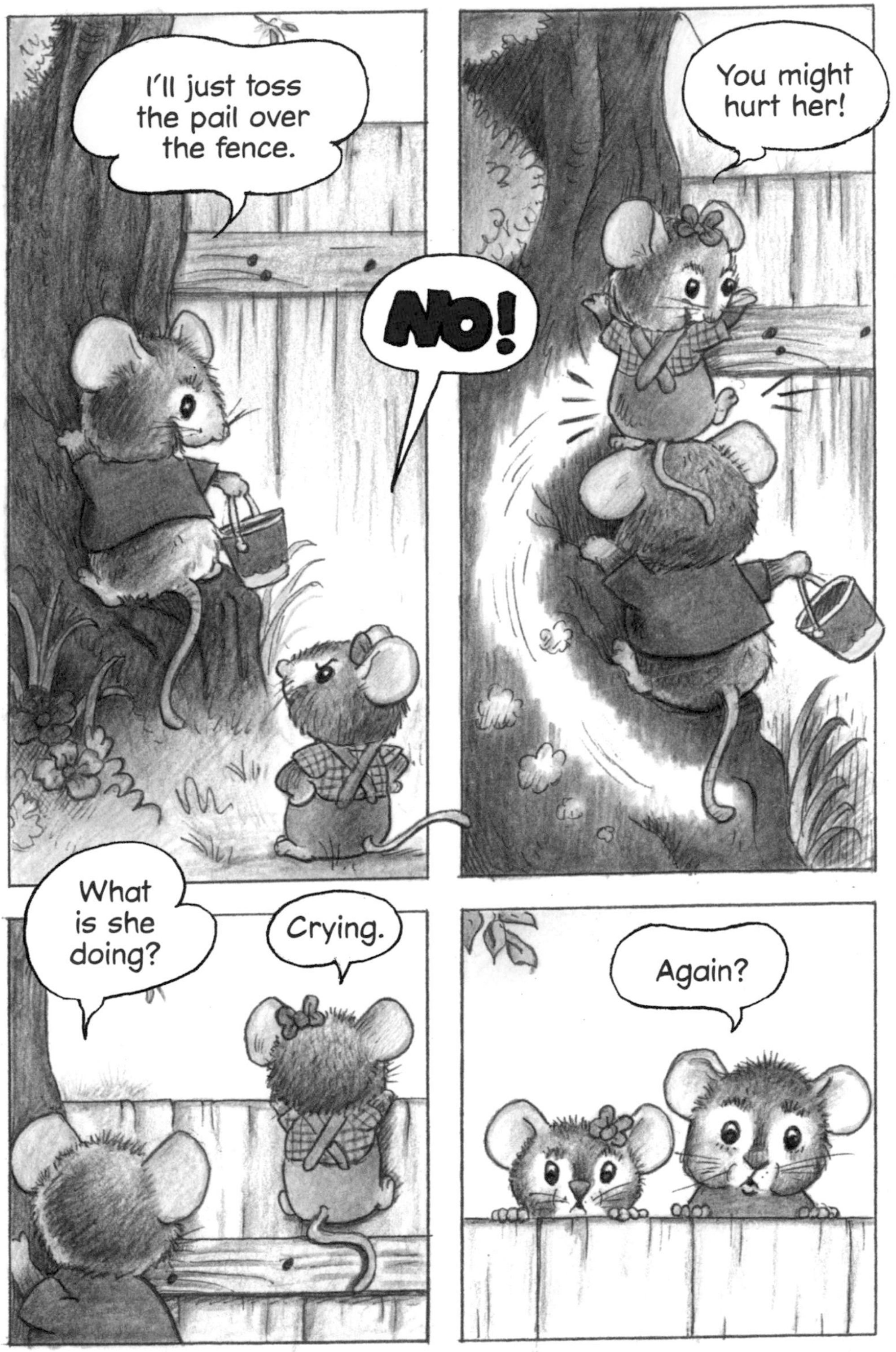
I'll just toss the pail over the fence.
NO!
You might hurt her!
What is she doing?
Crying.
Again?

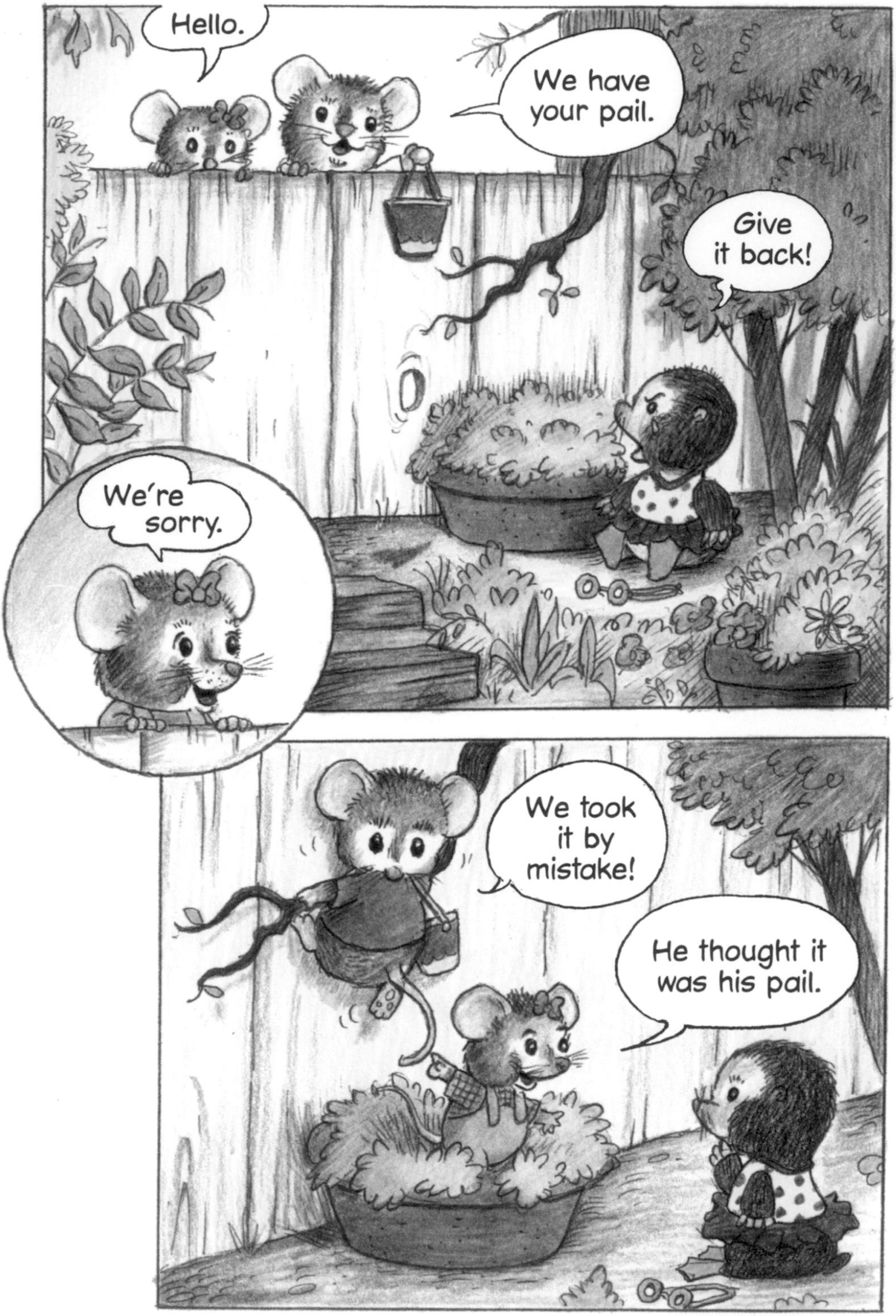
Hello.
We have your pail.
Give it back!
We're sorry.
We took it by mistake!
He thought it was his pail.

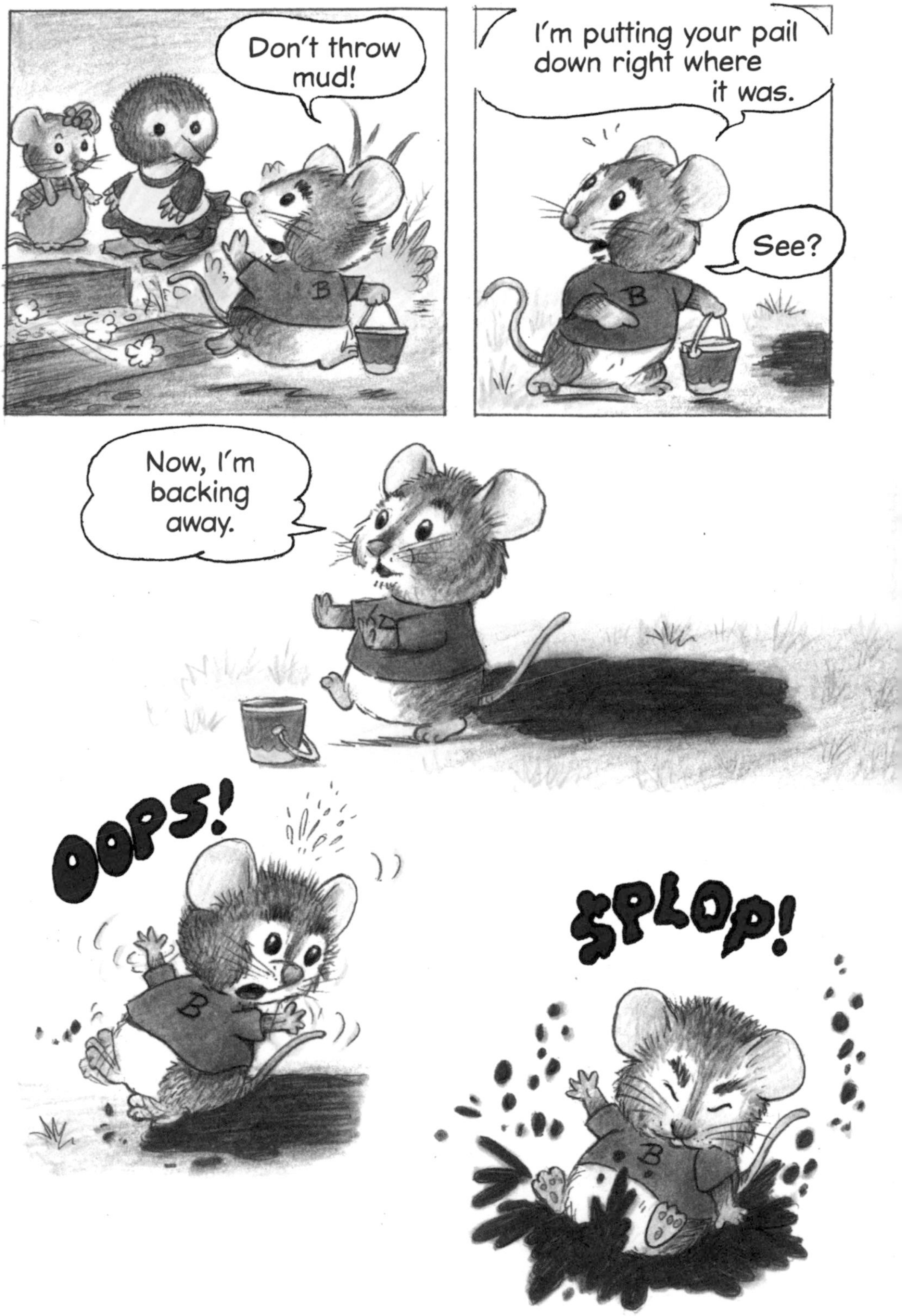
Don't throw mud!
I'm putting your pail down right where it was.
See?
Now, I'm backing away.
OOPS!
SPLOP!

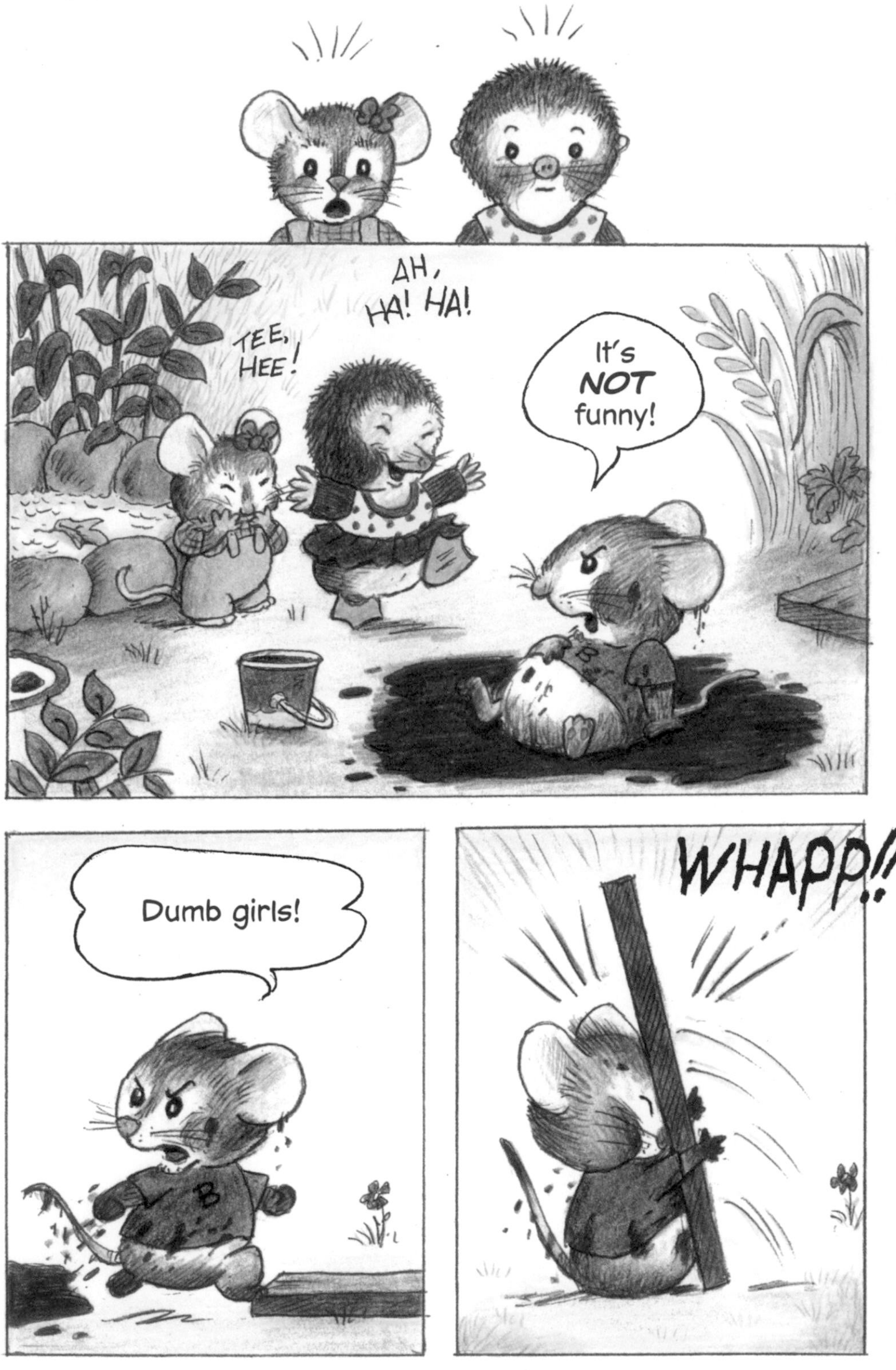
TEE, HEE!
AH, HA! HA!
It's **NOT** funny!
Dumb girls!
WHAPP!!

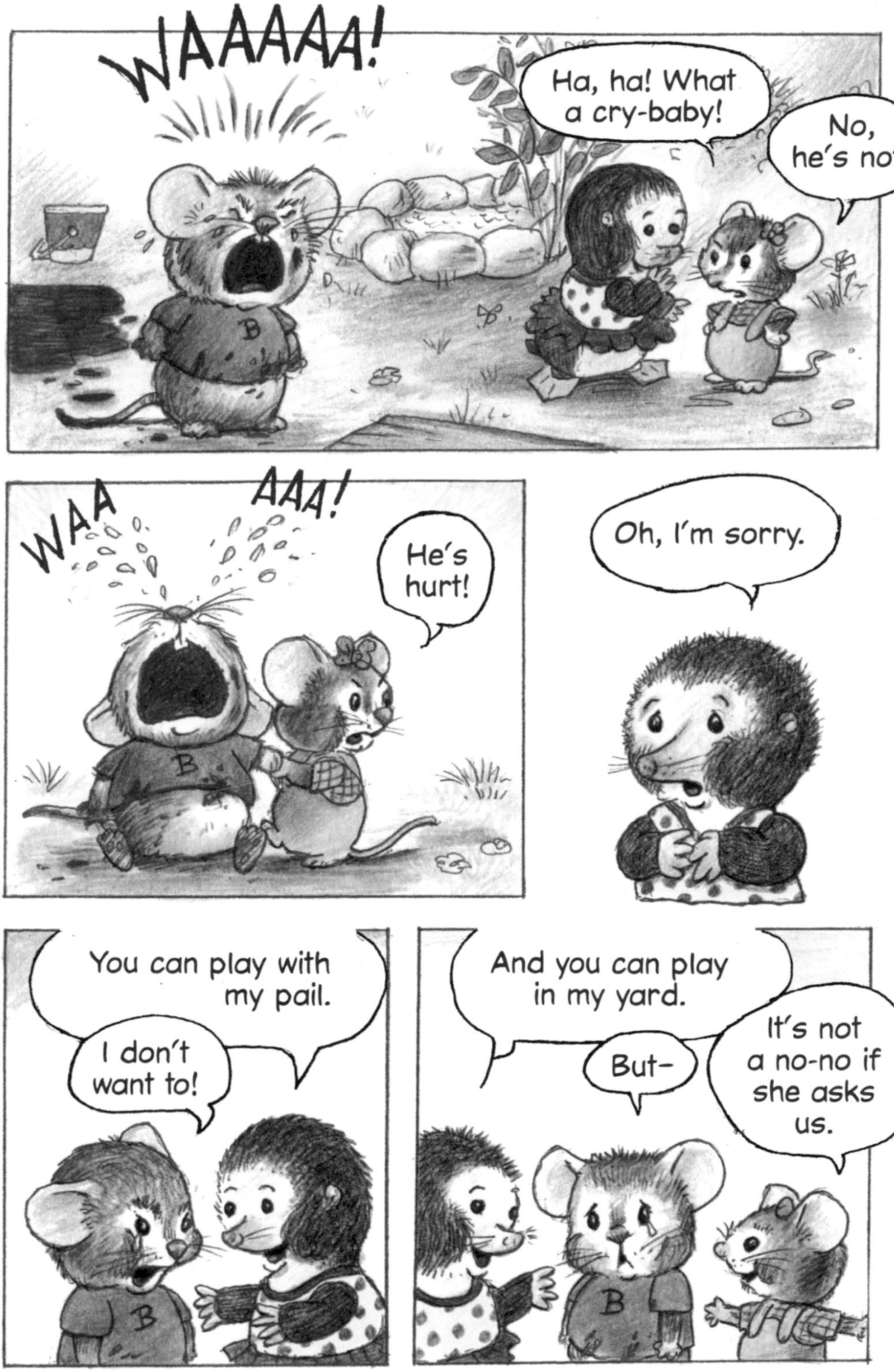
WAAAAA!
Ha, ha! What a cry-baby!
No, he's not!
WAA AAA!
He's hurt!
Oh, I'm sorry.
You can play with my pail.
I don't want to!
And you can play in my yard.
But–
It's not a no-no if she asks us.

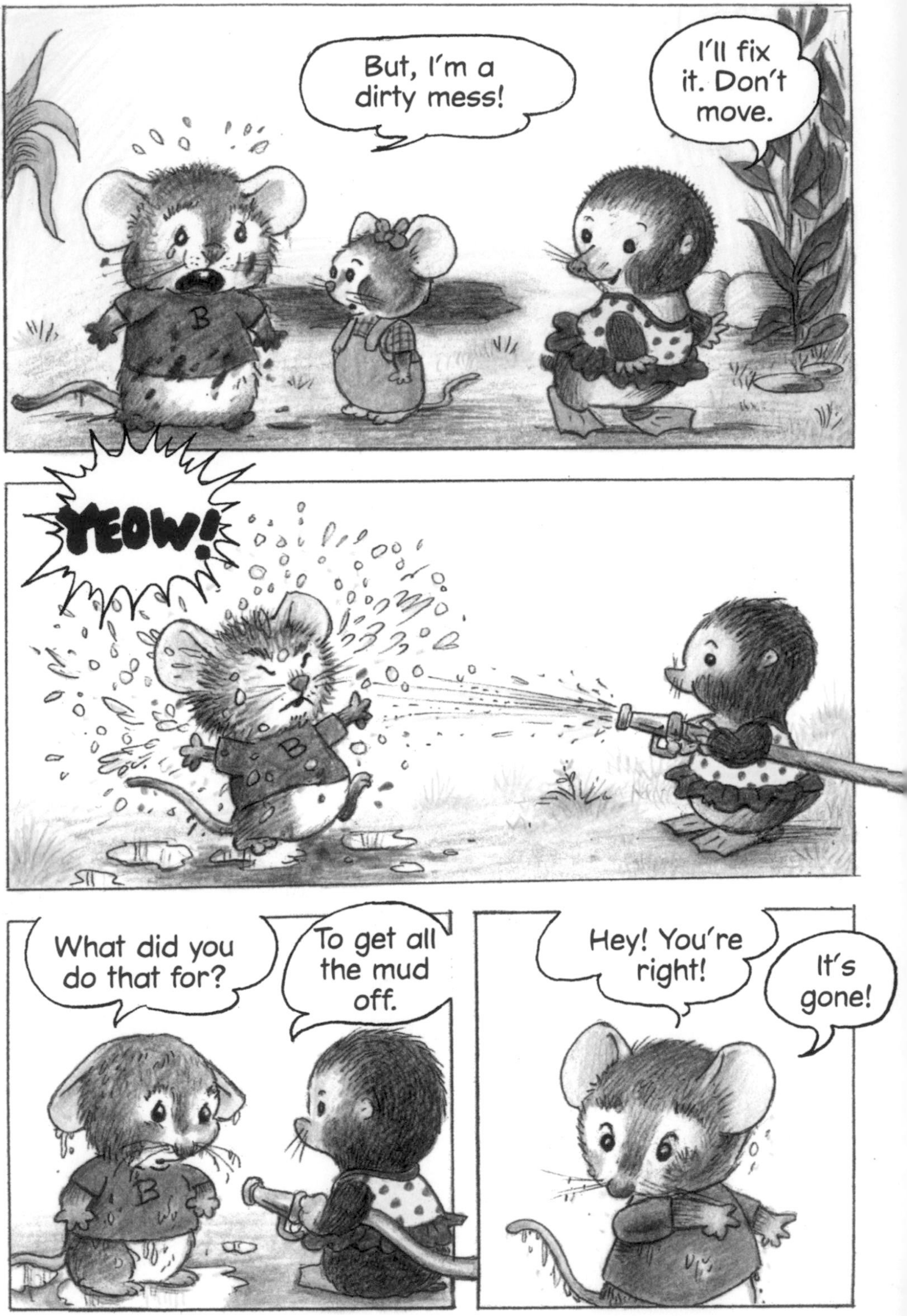
But, I'm a dirty mess!
I'll fix it. Don't move.
YEOW!
What did you do that for?
To get all the mud off.
Hey! You're right!
It's gone!

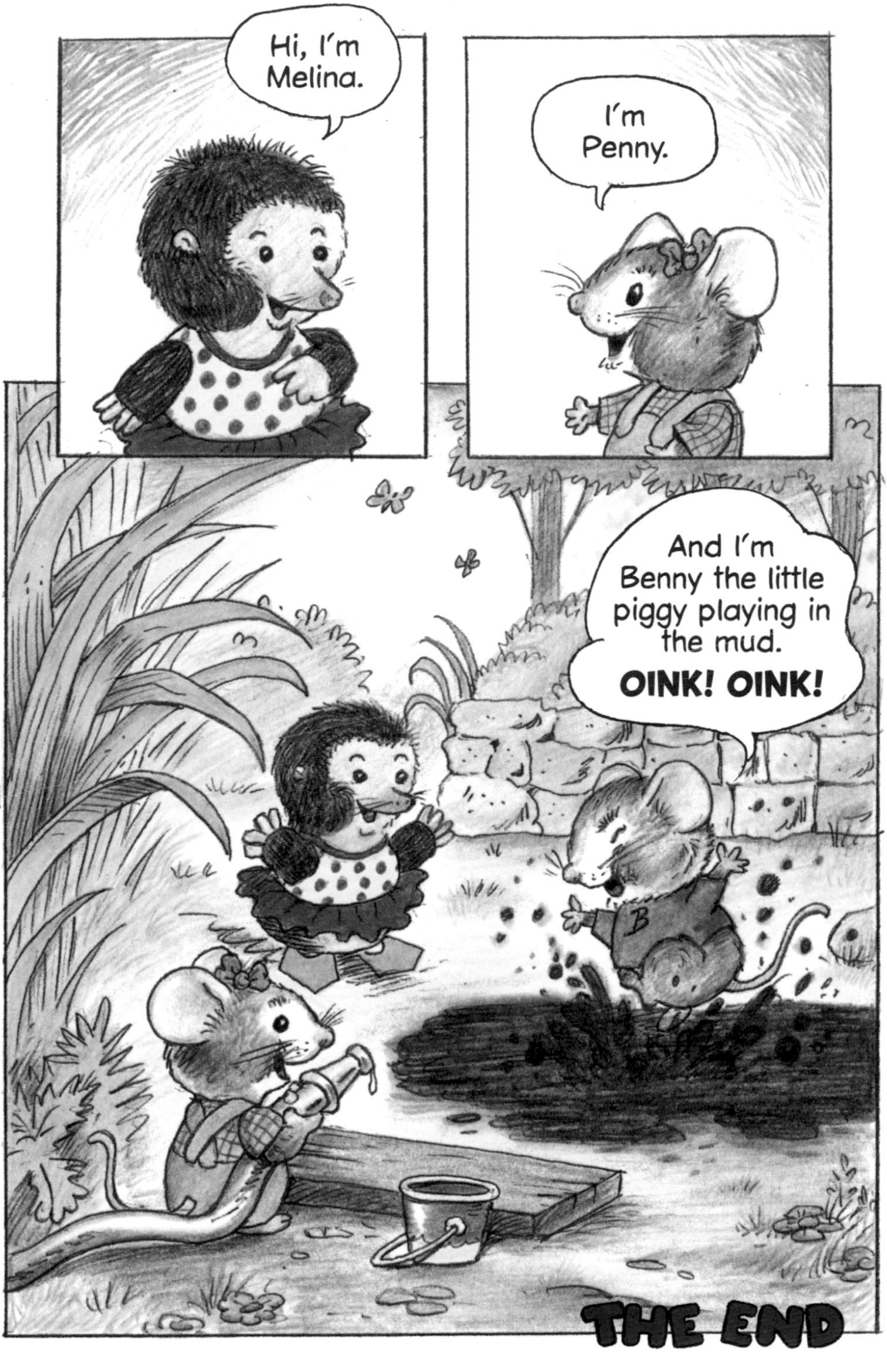
Hi, I'm Melina.
I'm Penny.
And I'm Benny the little piggy playing in the mud.
OINK! OINK!
THE END

ABOUT THE AUTHOR

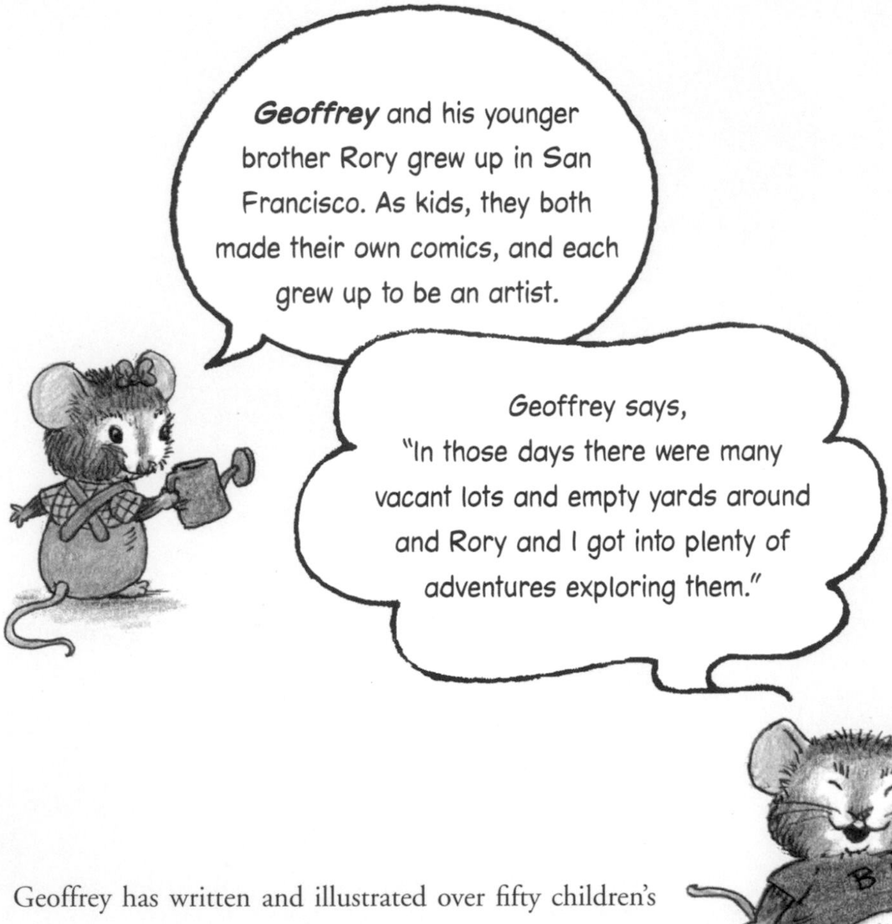
Geoffrey and his younger brother Rory grew up in San Francisco. As kids, they both made their own comics, and each grew up to be an artist.
Geoffrey says, "In those days there were many vacant lots and empty yards around and Rory and I got into plenty of adventures exploring them."

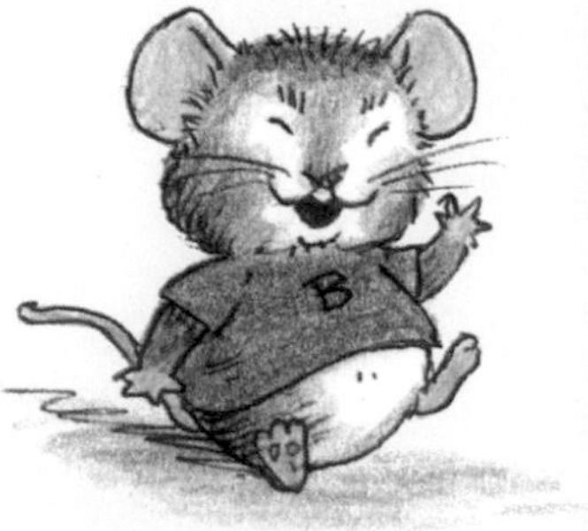

Geoffrey has written and illustrated over fifty children's books, including the extremely popular series of early readers *Otto and Uncle Tooth*, and *When the Wind Blew* by Caldecott Medal-winning author Margaret Wise Brown. He's beloved for his TOON Books – especially the Benny and Penny series, named "Best of Continuing Series"by Kirkus Reviews, and the Patrick Bear books. This book, *Benny and Penny in The Big No-No!,* received the 2010 Theodor Seuss Geisel award, an award given annually by the ALA's Association for Library Service to Children to the author of "the most distinguished American book for beginning readers published in the United States."

HOW TO "TOON INTO READING"
in a few simple steps:

Our goal is to get kids reading—and we know kids LOVE comics. We publish award-winning early readers in comics form for elementary and early middle school, and present them in three levels.

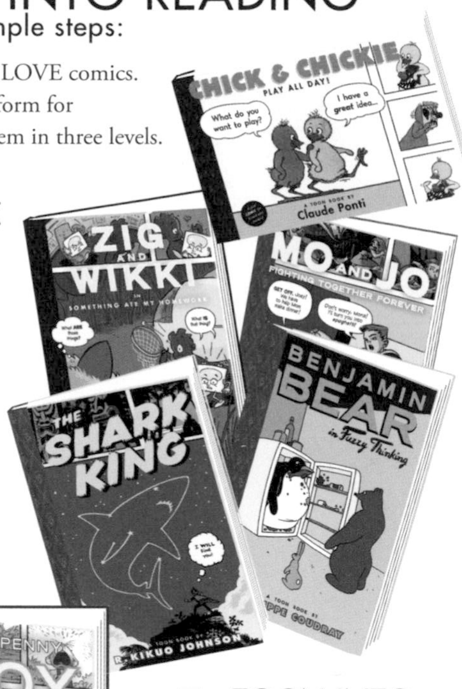
CHICK & CHICKIE
PLAY ALL DAY!
What do you want to play?
I have a great idea...
A TOON BOOK BY
Claude Ponti
ZIG AND WIKKI
SOMETHING ATE MY HOMEWORK
MO AND JO
FIGHTING TOGETHER FOREVER
BENJAMIN BEAR
in Fuzzy Thinking
THE SHARK KING
I WILL find you!
KIKUO JOHNSON

1 FIND THE RIGHT BOOK

Veteran teacher Cindy Rosado tells what makes a good book for beginning and struggling readers alike: "A vetted vocabulary, plenty of picture clues, repetition, and a clear and compelling story. Also, the book shouldn't be too easy—or the reader won't learn, but neither should it be too hard—or he or she may get discouraged."

The TOON INTO READING!™ program is designed for beginning readers and works wonders with reluctant readers.

Look for these other Benny & Penny books by Geoffrey Hayes:

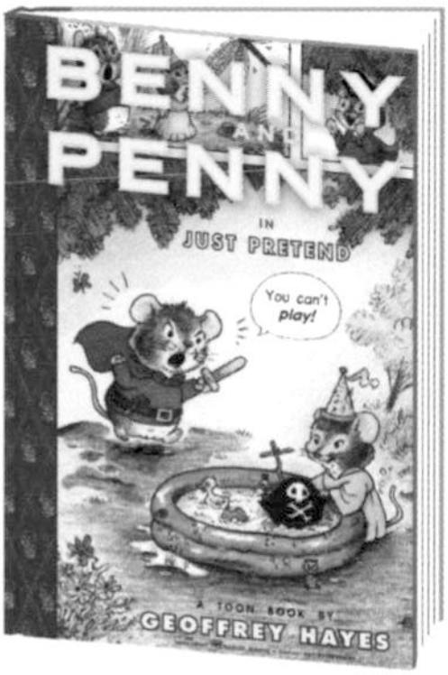
BENNY AND PENNY
IN
JUST PRETEND
You can't play!
A TOON BOOK BY
GEOFFREY HAYES

BENNY AND PENNY in Jusr Pretend

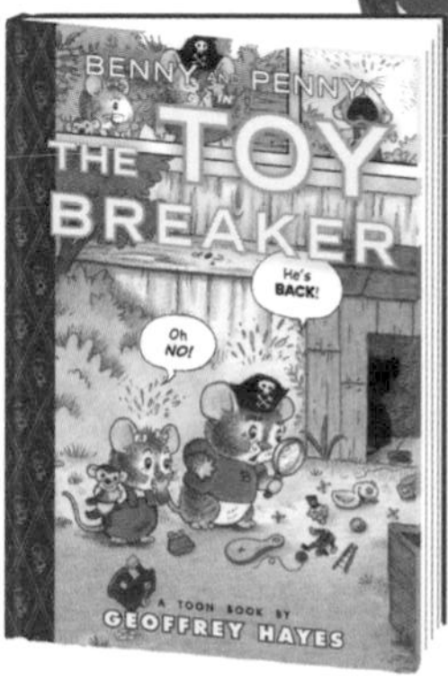
BENNY AND PENNY
THE TOY BREAKER
He's BACK!
Oh NO!
A TOON BOOK BY
GEOFFREY HAYES

BENNY AND PENNY in The Toy Breaker

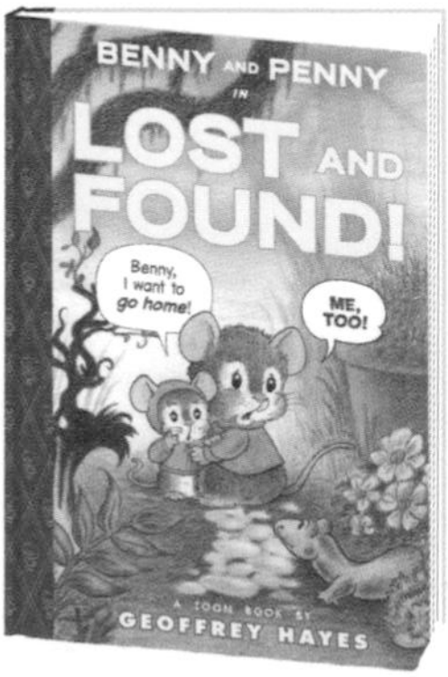
BENNY AND PENNY
IN
LOST AND FOUND!
Benny, I want to go home!
ME, TOO!
A TOON BOOK BY
GEOFFREY HAYES

BENNY AND PENNY in Lost and Found!

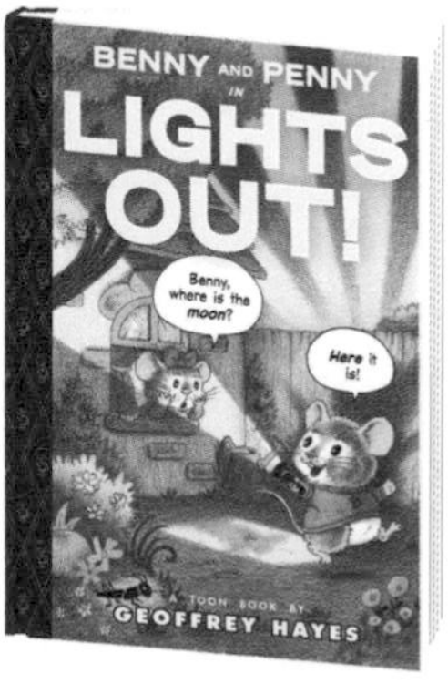
BENNY AND PENNY
IN
LIGHTS OUT!
Benny, where is the moon?
Here it is!
A TOON BOOK BY
GEOFFREY HAYES

BENNY AND PENNY in Lights Out!

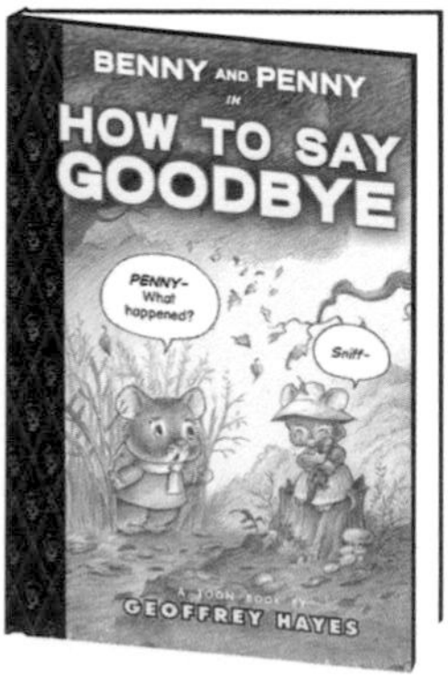
BENNY AND PENNY
IN
HOW TO SAY GOODBYE
PENNY- What happened?
Sniff-
A TOON BOOK BY
GEOFFREY HAYES

BENNY AND PENNY in How to Say Goodbye

What works?

Keep your fingertip <u>below</u> the character that is speaking.

2 GUIDE YOUNG READERS

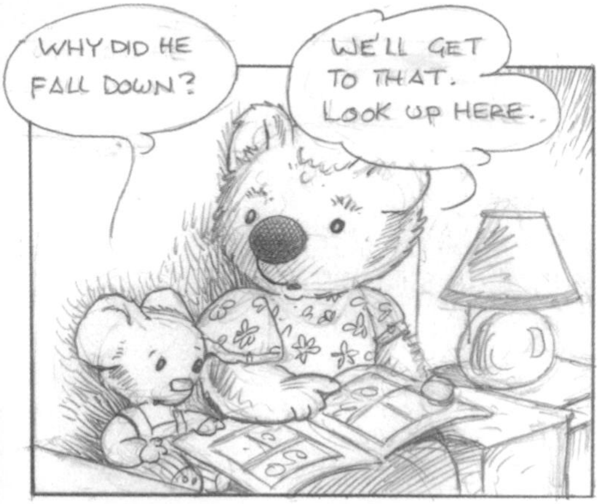
WHY DID HE FALL DOWN?
WE'LL GET TO THAT. LOOK UP HERE.

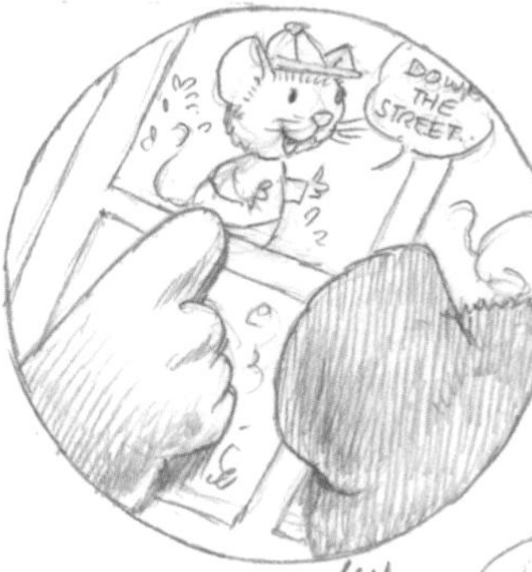
THE STREET.

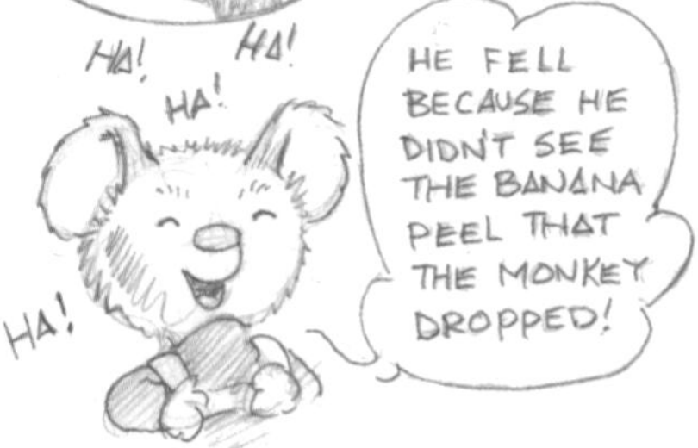
HA! HA! HA! HA!
HE FELL BECAUSE HE DIDN'T SEE THE BANANA PEEL THAT THE MONKEY DROPPED!

3 LET THE PICTURES TELL THE STORY

In a comic, you can often read the story even if you don't know all the words. Encourage young readers to tell you what's happening based on the facial expressions and body language.

4 GET OUT THE CRAYONS

Kids see the hand of the author in a comic and it makes them want to tell their own stories. Encourage them to talk, write and draw!

Get kids talking, and you'll be surprised at how perceptive they are about pictures.

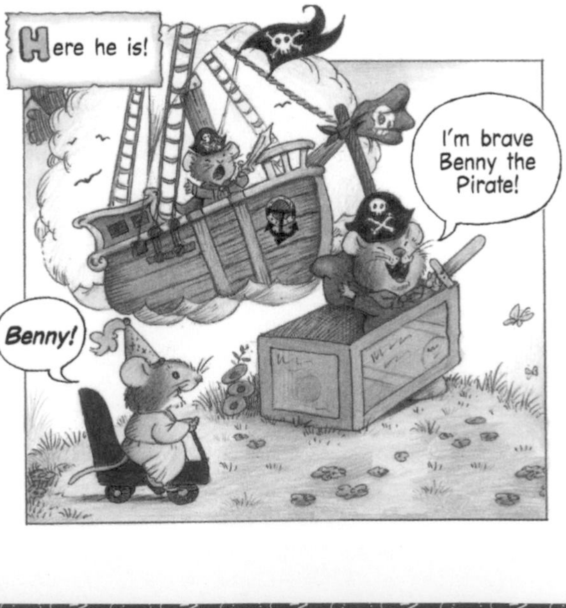
Here he is!
I'm brave Benny the Pirate!
Benny!

5 LET THEM GUESS

Comics provide a large amount of context for the words, so let young readers make informed guesses, and don't over-correct. In this panel, the artist shows a pirate ship, two pirate hats, and two pirate flags the first time the word "PIRATE" is introduced.